Also by Janwillem van de Wetering

FICTION
The Grijpstra-de Gier series:

Outsider in Amsterdam
Tumbleweed
The Corpse on the Dike
Death of a Hawker
The Japanese Corpse
The Blond Baboon
The Maine Massacre
Mind Murders
Streetbird
Rattle-Rat
The Sergeant's Cat (short stories)
Hard Rain

OTHER:
Inspector Saito's Small Satori
The Butterfly Hunter
Bliss and Bluster
The Safe Feeling
Murder by Remote Control

AUTOBIOGRAPHY
The Empty Mirror: Experiences in a Japanese Zen Monastery
A Glimpse of Nothingness: Experiences in an American
  Zen Community

BIOGRAPHY
Robert van Gulik, His Life, His Work

CHILDREN'S BOOKS
Hugh Pine
Hugh Pine and the Good Place
Hugh Pine and Something Else
Little Owl

Just a

Corpse at
Twilight

A Grijpstra & De Gier Mystery

Just a

Corpse at
Twilight

Janwillem van de Wetering

Published by
Soho Press Inc.
853 Broadway
New York, NY 10003

Library of Congress Cataloging-in-Publication Data

Van de Wetering, Janwillem, 1931–
[Drijflijk. English]
Just a corpse at twilight / Janwillem van de Wetering.
p.   cm.
"A substantially similar novel entitled Drijflijk © 1993 was
previously published in Dutch"—T.p. verso.
ISBN 1–56947–075–8
PT5881.32.A5D7513 1994

839.3′ 1364—dc30   94–9499
                                                 CIP

Book design by Cheryl L. Cipriani

Manufactured in the United States

10 9 8 7 6 5 4

Just a

Corpse at

Twilight

All our intelligent solutions are temporary and are only valid for a particular attack, not for the entire war between good and evil.

—*Isaac Bashevis Singer,* The Penitent

. . . that it doesn't just happen to people . . . but that it gets them closer related. . . .

—*from an interview with Abram de Swaan, Dutch author and sociologist*

Chapter 1

Henk Grijpstra, private detective, a portly fifty-odd-year-old in a pinstriped three-piece suit, drove home to his girlfriend Nellie's slender gable house on the Straight Tree Canal, inner city, Amsterdam, The Netherlands, where he lived and had his office.

Grijpstra felt contented: He had done a good job that day. It hadn't been much of a job, entailing the pacification of a smalltime blackmailer who had been worrying a smalltime merchant, but once again it had been Grijpstra's own job, a job he could have refused. Although his resignation from the Amsterdam Municipal Police dated back over two years now, there hadn't been a day since he'd been self-employed that Grijpstra hadn't congratulated himself on his exceptional good luck. He could send prospective clients home now, he could say "Well, sir, this isn't *quite* my cup of tea." Grijpstra could also, if he wanted to be polite, recommend the competition. He didn't even have to cite reasons for refusing commissions. There would be reasons, of course: There was a certain type of client's arrogance Grijpstra was allergic to, and he never worked on divorces or other love-related entanglements. "What's love anyway?" Grijpstra would ask his beloved Nellie. He would raise a finger. "I'll tell you what love is. Love is a fart in a brown paper bag." He wouldn't lower the finger until she nodded agreement.

Nellie, smiling sweetly, would make coffee, cut cake, carry in the cat, anything to get HenkieLuvvie off the subject. Nellie liked love entanglements herself. Apart from the romantic aspect there was income involved and surely she and Grijpstra needed a good constant cash flow. Would he just look at her fully automated five-story mansion, his fuel-guzzling American four-wheel drive, at his monthly journeys to luxurious Luxembourg, would he just think of the *cost?*

"But, HenkieLuvvie," Nellie wailed whenever she heard a disgruntled client slam her recently restored antique front door. "Don't we *need* the money?"

"All will be well in the end." Grijpstra, with a wide gesture, would flick all demons of need away. "Don't worry about your worries."

Grijpstra, allowing his full-size Ford Bronco to run amber traffic lights, smiled. He thought of his many years in the Amsterdam Municipal Police, the "yessir years," as his former partner, Detective-Sergeant Rinus de Gier, now called them. Cops can't refuse jobs, they're ordered about by superiors. Adjutant Grijpstra and Sergeant de Gier, the Murder Brigade's most respected team, working under a famous chief of detectives, could never refuse a case. It wasn't just the chief, the old "commissaris" who ordered them about, it was also the Dutch superego, Holland's sense of righteousness, the frame of national conscience within which adjutant and sergeant acted. Grijpstra and de Gier often dreamed of being free of morals imposed by bureaucratic rules.

Grijpstra also dreamed of owning his own car. Like the freedom dream itself, the dream vehicle was outrageous. Grijpstra, in all his working years, what with obese Mrs. Grijpstra and the voracious kids, could never afford a private car.

"Can you afford your dreams?" the commissaris would ask. He would pat Grijpstra's shoulder. "Adjutant, once dreams come true, so do their consequences. Can you live with what desire will drag along for you?"

Private Detective Grijpstra smiled. Here independent, affluent Grijpstra was, driving his very own gleaming blue-and-white vehicle, high on big wheels. Grijpstra felt pleased that quiet summer evening in the big car's majestic driver's seat as he looked down on pitiful compacts, scurrying mopeds, pathetic pedestrians. Wasn't the Grijpstrayan universe, for the moment anyway, just hunky-dory?

Could he make hunky-doriness last?

Grijpstra gripped the wheel as his body swayed, prey to an abdominal cramp, to what felt like a sharp-snouted beetle gnawing about for a moment, an inch behind his navel. Grijpstra remembered the beetle, it had warned him before.

Grijpstra drove on, considering possibilities.

Was he about to lose something? What did he own that money couldn't replace? His health? He didn't mind getting sick; Nellie would serve him gourmet foods on the little tray table that fit across his legs, fluff his pillows, change the sheets. He could read, watch videos, look through his bird books. Losing his detective license would be just fine too—perhaps it was time to live in the country, potter about, maybe fish in a quiet tributary of the Amstel River. He had enough to do: paint, play drums. Nellie? Grijpstra didn't think he would lose Nellie. Have an accident, lose his life? No more Grijpstra to worry about. No more Grijpstra?

The beetle bit again, briefly, almost making Grijpstra lose control of the wheel.

Grijpstra parked the Bronco in the expensive rental garage around the corner, strolled home, got kissed by Nellie and purred at by Tabriz. Tabriz, an oversize cat with a coat like a well-worn Oriental carpet, had once belonged to former Detective-Sergeant de Gier. De Gier, who, like Grijpstra, had announced his resignation at the commissaris's retirement party some two years ago, had been traveling since then. He lived in America now, on the deserted coast of Maine, on his own rented island, where he happily pursued a philosophical quest. De Gier, ten years younger than Grijpstra, more intellectual, taller, athletic, and a talented amateur jazz trumpet player, had taken time out in order to grasp the point of it all.

"Good riddance," Nellie would say to her newfound friend, Katrien, "to bad rubbish. . . . Oh, sorry, Henkie-Luvvie, I never know whether you're in the room or not. I wish you wouldn't move about so quietly, dear."

Katrien was the wife of the retired commissaris.

Grijpstra's beetle, pushed back by beef tongue and caper stew on noodles, a Nellie specialty that came with a spinach salad, hardly moved about now. Grijpstra, relieved, was about to sit down on the couch for his after-dinner espresso when the beetle bit again, just as the telephone rang.

Grijpstra, massaging his stomach, pointed his nose at the phone. "You take it, Nellie."

"HenkieLuvvie," Nellie said from the couch "Please. It's after nine. It'll be a client."

The beetle tore at Grijpstra's intestine. Grijpstra, trying to deal with the animal's onslaught, waited for the answering machine to click on.

"Henk?" the answering machine's little speaker asked plaintively.

Grijpstra sighed and picked up the phone. *Rinus,* he should have said joyfully. His old pal phoning all the way from America, how nice. *How're you doing, old buddy? Good to hear you. Everything okay?* Grijpstra didn't say any of that.

"Yes," Grijpstra said coldly.

"Oh dear," Nellie said.

"I am in deep shit," de Gier said.

"Tell me about it," Grijpstra said.

De Gier reported.

Grijpstra and de Gier had been cops together for years. Then, a few words sufficed to clarify a situation, but that was in the past. De Gier was a private citizen now.

"You're kidding," Grijpstra said.

De Gier wasn't kidding.

"What's up?" Nellie asked, watching TV.

Grijpstra covered the phone's mouthpiece. "Rinus says he killed a woman. The idiot kicked her down some cliffs. Must have been drunk. Stoned maybe."

Grijpstra, his hand still on the phone, looked peaceful enough, with his back to a window in Nellie's cozy sitting room, sitting on the armrest of her couch. Behind him elm trees on the canal's quay slowly waved their branches, looking like comforting holy men's arms in wide sleeves woven from countless fresh green leaves. A sea gull flying close to the house briefly filled the window's frame. Geraniums blossomed on the wide windowsill, the middle plant glowing deep red, the other two pink.

"Not really, right?" Nellie asked. She looked back to the screen—her evening images were never real, not even when the news readers showed the misery of famine, crime, or war.

"Not really, right?" Grijpstra asked across the Atlantic.

"Yes, *really*, wrong."

De Gier's reality was a jetty on the coast of Maine,

where he screened his eyes from a cloudless sky above an energetically foaming Bay of Fundy. The turbulent water reflected harsh daylight because, given the earth's restless rotations, the East Coast of the United States is still going strong six hours after Western Europe's day is over.

De Gier was telephoning from the fishing village of Jameson, Maine. The battered pay phone, center of a random design of scratched and written numbers, was attached to a weathered board on the outside wall of Jameson's only restaurant, Beth's Diner. The diner was housed in a ramshackle building, still elegant in its old age, surrounded by a gallery of chiseled slender posts under a moss-and-lichen-covered shingled roof. The restaurant's overall color had become silver-gray within peeling baby blue framing. Rotted-out gingerbread decorations and cornerposts sculpted long ago to resemble Greek pillars witnessed past glory, dating back to Jameson's days as a real port, when it had wharfs where clipper ships were built for the China trade, when the town was the hub of a worldwide lumber business, when it exported granite cut out of the islands, the building blocks of America's big cities. Now there was only lobstering, with crabbing on the side (as long as they were in the lobster traps anyway), and just a touch of tourism, accidental mostly, for Jameson was well away from any beaten track. There were some old folks too, in RVs or trailers hiding behind cedar fences, snowbirds who were gone before the autumn colors faded. Then there were oddballs "from away," like Rinus de Gier, who, since his resignation from the Amsterdam police force two years back, had been without a fixed address or a known source of income.

"De Gier is playing Indians on his own," Grijpstra once told Nellie during a leisurely Sunday breakfast beneath the flowering vines in her backyard. Grijpstra had hypothesized a possible midlife crisis, arguing that de Gier lived a solitary life, refusing to accept responsibility for wife and kiddies, and therefore had not grown up, so he'd been hit by his midlife crisis later. Nellie had smiled. "Clever Henkie-Luvvie."

"So will you come?" de Gier now asked across the Atlantic. "To help out your old buddy? If you please?"

"That nature woman on the island next door," Grijpstra, his hand on the mouthpiece again, told Nellie. "Her name was Lorraine. He mentioned her to Katrien. Katrien showed you the letter."

There was a couple kissing on-screen. Nellie switched the TV to mute, she never liked to listen to kissing.

"I thought . . . weren't those two happy?" Nellie asked. She wanted love to last, for herself and for everyone she knew. She was with Henk now, sharing what used to be Nellie's hotel, now formally closed down after she finally popped her reluctant lover—couldn't His Loveship be stubborn?—from his old apartment at the Tanning Canal. Grijpstra had suffered in overstuffed rooms at the Tanning Canal with his wife, and been happy, without his wife, in empty rooms, visiting Nellie from time to time. He had still been in the police then, paying alimony and rent. Money still counted then. Nellie had offered a free room; Grijpstra, reluctant at the time, agreed. Now that there was Grijpstra's Private Agency, and a lot of money all of a sudden, Nellie no longer took in guests. Things were getting better and better.

"Rinus really murdered her?" Nellie asked.

The TV station slipped into a commercial. Nellie remoted beautiful actors who were shoving a rhinoceros aside with their imported pickup to wherever it was remoted beautiful actors go when their screen gets switched off. So this was real trouble? Nellie didn't think Rinus would joke about killing off Nature Woman.

"You're not really going anywhere?" Nellie asked.

"I'm not really going anywhere?" Grijpstra echoed.

De Gier, an ocean away, studied his handful of American quarters, three times the size of their Dutch counterparts. He inserted more quarters. The magnitude of the coins reminded him of the magnitude of his problem.

"Henk? You better come and help out here. I don't even remember what happened. Was Lorraine bothering me? Flash and Bad George say I kicked her. Apparently Lorraine fell, here on Squid Island, and hurt herself on the rocks, badly—she was bleeding. I did see blood on the cliff. I was about to perform this thing, this ceremony I was planning. All I remember is that Lorraine came to visit and that she was in the way."

"You don't remember hurting her?"

"I was drunk," de Gier offered, "as I said, and stoned. I've been experimenting with mixtures. I was about to play some music, a CD, jazz, Miles Davis, just got it in the mail. This was a ceremony, if you will, all set up. Well prepared in advance. Lorraine wasn't part of that. She kayaked in unannounced. She was bothering me."

"Ah," Grijpstra said.

"Lorraine messed with my ceremony, Henk."

"So you kicked her off the cliff and left her to bleed to death? *Jesus! Rinus!*"

"*Jesus Rinus* is right," de Gier said. "So will you come over, old buddy? This just happened. Nobody knows yet, except Flash and Bad George. They took away Lorraine's body late last night and presented a bill this morning. Got it, old buddy? You and me got a problem; we settle the problem. Okay? Okay."

"Blackmail?" Grijpstra asked, remembering the case he had just dealt with. His own bill wasn't as high as the charge his petty merchant had been facing. There had to be an incentive for all parties concerned.

He saw little incentive now. What if he carefully replaced the phone, loosened his waistcoat and necktie, laid down a newspaper on Nellie's new coffee table, put his feet on the paper, lit a Cuban cigar—pity he had quit smoking— sipped iced jenever—pity he had quit drinking. What if he said, "Fuck you, Rinus, fuck your little voice whining across a large ocean, we're happy here.'"

"Henk? Hello?" the little voice whined.

"Right here," Grijpstra said. "Tell me about Flash and Bad George, the parties who witnessed this murder."

"They didn't," de Gier said.

"So how did they know you were kicking Victim?"

"Victim told them. She was still alive when they found her."

"Describe your accusers."

"Flash is Flash Farnsworth, Bad George is just Bad George. They're skippers of the *Kathy Three,* a junk boat that runs errands between Jameson and the islands. The boat is named after a dog. All I have is a dinghy so I call them by radio if I need anything big. If I don't call they show up anyway; they're kind of friendly, cute, two small-sized guys. They usually come by once a day and if I need them I wave. Last night they were late."

"Flash is bad too?"

"Flash and Bad George aren't too bad," de Gier said. "They're more like silly. Flash has felted hair, like a bird's nest. Bad George had a car accident, his face got stitched up by a cheap doctor who changed it into a doll's face. They're simpletons who live on their vessel with their smart dog, Kathy Two. They came back this morning, after getting rid of Lorraine's body, to get paid off."

"Don't tell me you paid."

"I said I was light on change," de Gier said, "but that you'd help out. Okay?"

"So the law doesn't know yet?"

"No."

"You have choices," Grijpstra said. "You know that, don't you?"

"I pay?" de Gier asked. "I choose to kick Flash and Bad George down the cliffs too? I choose to go to jail? Jail isn't pretty here, Henk. Inmates watch a dead screen all afternoon, until the guard comes to push the button for the evening news."

"You could run," Grijpstra said pleasantly. "Just *ease* yourself away." His sweeping hand illustrated the image.

"It'll ease after me," de Gier said. "Besides, I have to know what happened here."

"Remember what we used to tell suspects?" Grijpstra asked. "When we were out of cells again?"

" 'Run, asshole, run'?" de Gier asked. "No. Listen. This is Jameson, Woodcock County, state of Maine. You can find it. Fly in via Boston. Take El Al. I just phoned, they've got a flight leaving Schiphol Airport at two A.M. your time. Out of Boston there should be a commuter flight to Portland. Rent a car from there. It'll take just a few hours."

"*You* pick me up."

"I can't," de Gier said. "There's too much going on here. I'm very visible. The sheriff might put out an all-points."

"I get sleepy driving," Grijpstra said.

"You still have that trouble?"

"Getting worse." Grijpstra nodded. "But I know why now—I have these polyps that grow in my sinuses that make me snore and wake up at night. Don't get enough rest. If we go out of town Nellie has to drive me."

"Get operated on."

"Sure," Grijpstra said. "There's a two-month waiting list. Keep me informed meanwhile. Let me know how you're doing. Goodbye for now, Rinus."

"HENK!"

"Right here."

"Take the bus from Portland to Jameson. It's a Greyhound. It's easy, Henk."

"I'll get lost," Grijpstra said. "You're the international type, not me, remember?"

"Ask the commissaris for directions," de Gier said. "He and I were here before when he had to help his widowed sister.

"HELLO?" de Gier called, breaking the silence.

"I'm on my own now," Grijpstra said.

"I'm sorry, Henk."

"You don't sound sorry."

"But I am."

"You shouldn't kick friendly women to death," Grijpstra said.

"Squid Island," de Gier said, forced by his diminishing stock of coins to talk quickly. "With your back to Beth's Diner that'll be the second island off the peninsula on your left. The island with the pedestal house, lots of glass under two kind of peaked sloping roofs. Like a pagoda, you can't miss it. At rowing distance from the Point. Have Beth—she owns the restaurant, she's a friend—or Aki call the *Kathy Three* on the citizens band radio. Flash and Bad George will pick you up. Stay away from the sheriff, Hairy Harry."

"Who?"

"Joke," de Gier said. "Hairy Harry's hair never grew." Through a window next to his phone booth de Gier could see the sheriff inside the restaurant. Hairy Harry was a pleasant enough looking man but a poor-quality window pane distorted his bare skull, made it pointed, so that he looked like a space character out of a badly drawn cartoon. Extraterrestrial Hairy Harry was munching a hamburger, with a double helping of trimmings. The sheriff wore a faded checkered flannel shirt, neatly ironed, and patched but clean jeans stuck into polished half-high boots. His bit of a belly might be more muscle than flab. A long-barreled Magnum revolver in a holster was held up by a polished police-type gun belt, with handcuffs, notebook, and flashlight all neatly inserted. The sheriff raised a hand to greet de Gier, then dropped it to force a stream of honey into his coffee. The honey oozed from an upside-down transparent bear-shaped plastic squeeze bottle. Honeybear's feet looked puny above the sheriff's pink fist.

Grijpstra said, "No one saw you even kick the alleged victim. So, no corpse, no murder."

De Gier's last quarters clashed into the phone. "No."

"Where's the body now?"

"My blackmailers hid it. Listen," de Gier said. "Picture the situation: I'm deliberately high on this whiskey-and-pot-and-Miles Davis combination. Lorraine arrives. She wants meaningful hanky-panky. I say, 'Some other evening, darling.' She still wants meaningful hanky-panky. Push comes to shove. And she must have fallen down that cliff. I go into the house. The motor vessel *Kathy Three* arrives, with Kathy Two on the bridge, barking like crazy. I see the ship, hear the dog, but I don't react. Flash and Bad George go ashore and find Lorraine, bleeding. Lorraine tells them I came at her and kicked her. Flash gets into the house but I'm too far gone to say anything. Flash takes a blanket from the house. He and Bad George wrap Lorraine in the blanket, carry her to the boat, and set off for Jameson to take her to a doctor. But halfway there, Lorraine dies. The *Kathy Three* turns back and Flash and George show me Lorraine's corpse. I'm still out of my mind. Flash suggests that he and George get rid of the corpse somewhere. I say sure."

"Kathy Two is a dog?"

"Small and woolly. She likes me. She liked Lorraine, too. Flash says they wouldn't have checked Squid Island last night if Kathy hadn't been barking. As soon as they got close, Kathy Two jumped ashore and led them to Lorraine."

"Who is Kathy One?"

"Mother of Flash Farnsworth. She gave him a bad time so he told her she'd have to come back as his dog. There's some Indian blood here; Indians believe in ideas like that."

"Flash treats the dog well?"

"Kathy Two runs his whole show."

"So Flash isn't all bad?"

"No," de Gier said. "But he thinks I'm made of money and he has this little notebook in the breast pocket of his overall and a little bit of a pencil and he likes to write bills.

He's been ripping me off for running errands but the man is poor and *Kathy Three* is expensive to run and it would be hard to get along here without the services of those two and I've got all this cash."

"What did Flash charge for getting rid of the body?"

"Ten thousand."

"Dollars?"

"Dollars is the currency here."

"So?"

"Okay," de Gier said, "I know what you're saying, but it's the principle, Henk."

A recorded message interfered, asking for more quarters.

"I'm out of coins. So you're coming, Henk? Okay?"

Grijpstra's answering okay got lost as the phone first clicked, then buzzed. The lack of communication, Grijpstra told Nellie afterward, didn't matter because he and de Gier were friends: Twenty years of togetherness form a connection for the duration. De Gier knew he could rely on his soulmate Grijpstra. He and de Gier had a spiritual relationship, a shared quest, if you will. De Gier took care of the subtle aspect of that quest while Grijpstra was in charge of basic details. Grijpstra told Nellie that such bonding might be hard to explain.

Nellie helped Grijpstra pack. She said he didn't have to explain because the whole thing was pure little boy's masturbation bullshit, that he'd been looking for an excuse to leave her for a while now, that he was just itching to chase more exotic women. She found his pistol, a Walther P 5, the new police weapon, no safety, unable not to demolish anything it pointed at (up to six hundred feet), but Grijpstra put the weapon back between the longjohns he wouldn't take along either. "Won't get through airport security, honey."

"Won't they try to hurt you out there?" Nellie's ample bosom, packed in a pink sweater, flowed against Grijpstra's powerful chest.

Nellie had been a Miss Holland contestant, but her attributes had overwhelmed the judges. Nellie lost, but her friendly pimp, university student Gerard, was the lucky winner. Nellie didn't love Gerard then but found it hard to resist his charm and good looks. Gerard, Nellie told her intimate friend Katrien not all that long ago, when they were having tea, resembled de Gier, both in- and outside. Gerard and Rinus could be twins. Here we see two very similar men, one dead, one drifting, both tall, athletic, philosophically curious, sporting cavalry mustaches, surrealists who refuse to watch TV, not even football. Gerard read modern French literature aloud to please Nellie, whose parents were Belgian/French, but the existentialist French authors depressed Nellie and the literary French authors seemed too clever, and both brands finished up interfering with her well-earned sleep. De Gier was reputed to read French nihilism to his cats. "*Toutes les valeurs sont vides, Oliver. On ne connaît rien, Tabriz.*" De Gier excelled in judo. Gerard liked fencing. Both men drank some, but a pimp is subject to less discipline than a policeman, so Gerard drank

more. There was a bar fight and Gerard got knifed by a
colleague. Nellie thanked the Lord at Gerard's funeral, after
she stole his savings. The devout former mistress set up a
private hotel, with champagne room service for gentleman
guests, to pay off the mortgage.

"How did you meet Adjutant Grijpstra, dear?" Katrien
had asked.

Detective-Adjutant Grijpstra had been in charge of the
investigation of Gerard's violent death.

"Nothing to do with you?" Katrien asked.

Katrien and Nellie had been having tea at Katrien's
house, facing the Queen's Boulevard in Amsterdam's fash-
ionable southern quarter. Katrien, from the rear veranda,
kept an eye on her husband. The commissaris puttered about
in his garden, wafting away gasoline fumes with vigorous
sweeps of his cane, keeping clean a row of lettuce that he
grew for his pet, a turtle.

"Nothing to do with me." Nellie smiled.

"The Lord helped out," Katrien said. She had no faith
but she was the hostess of this tea party. And there was the
class difference too, Katrien being titled and Nellie a retired
whore. Katrien didn't want to be awkward.

Gerard being dead, both women concentrated on the
living.

"Rinus is no good either," Nellie said, "and he would
have been as bad if the commissaris hadn't taught him."

Katrien wasn't sure. Gerard could have found his commissaris too, had he tried.

"You think Gerard didn't want to learn?" Nellie asked. "But he did. He was always studying some book or other. On his own. Wasn't that sort of . . ."

". . . admirable," Katrien said. "Yes. But my husband, Jan, never tried to boss his colleagues. He didn't dominate de Gier in any way, I mean."

"Even so," Nellie said. "You know Grijpstra? My HenkieLuvvie? He's always quoting your Jan. 'The commissaris used to say this. The commissaris used to say that.'"

"I know," Katrien said. "My Jan quotes ancient Greeks."

"A man has to know his own mind."

"Men don't have their own minds," Katrien said.

That was funny. They laughed.

Nellie wanted to say something nice too. "And de Gier never lived off women."

Katrien broke open a can of chocolate-coated wafers. Hostess and guest munched and Katrien said that she was sorry, now that she was old, and the commissaris retired, and the whole thing was over, so to speak, that she had never worked. She had studied law, graduated with honors, could have practiced, but she had had kids instead.

"That's nice too," Nellie said.

"You like kids?" Katrien asked.

"I only had customers," Nellie said. "And HenkieLuvvie now, but I would sometimes like to have a real baby."

"Funny," Katrien said, "I used to like babies too but now they all look like grubs to me."

They laughed.

"How many grubs did you have?" Nellie asked.

"Too many," Katrien said. "Then look what happens: Nine hundred Dutchmen to the square mile, and three of them are mine, three too many."

"How many Dutchmen should there be to the square mile?" Nellie asked.

"None?" Katrien replied.

"It works both ways," Grijpstra told Nellie now. He told her about male friendship being a thing of beauty, about total trust, about the covenant of the Secret Knights. Suppose he, Grijpstra, were in trouble now. All he'd have to do would be to flick his fingers and there would be Sir Rinus de Gier, jumping in full armor out of the nearest closet, firing an Uzi. Wiping out Neo-Nazis. Risking everything to save old Grijpstra.

"Don't help him out for free," Nellie said. "Rinus is loaded." She pushed Grijpstra's chest. "How come Rinus is loaded?"

"Inheritance?" Grijpstra asked. "His mother?"

"Please," Nellie said.

Grijpstra towered over Nellie, explaining Rinus's wealth. "First de Gier's mother passed away, then his sister died too, she turned black with cancer, so de Gier got his mother's house and savings and his sister's antique needle-work collection that he auctioned off for big bucks. Then he overheard some investment bankers in the elevator and made a killing on the stock exchange, subsequently doubling that killing in a casino. Lucky Rinus!"

"Sure," Nellie said. She knew better than to argue. How many times does a pittance have to multiply to pay for travels to New Guinea (where on earth is New Guinea?), to stay with Papuan headhunters for eighteen months, meanwhile popping up for weekends in Amsterdam, for skipping off to America afterward, for sending photographs of self in sports cars (nobody rents out sports cars), on motorcycles (you have to buy motorcycles too), in new safari suits, with beauties (beauties don't come cheap). Whoever heard of a gambler risking his wad and not losing his wad?

"De Gier earned regular money in New Guinea," Grijpstra said. "He didn't just study with that voodoo fellow, he also assisted the police commissioner of Port Moresby. That very subtle Japanese case? The diplomat murder? Remember all the faxes Rinus sent? And I bet the Japanese Embassy in Port Moresby paid him too."

"Sure." Nellie smiled sweetly. She'd been a whore and whores are smart. Since when are guest police officers well paid in Third World countries?

"You're just jealous," Grijpstra laughed. He blocked Nellie's left hook.

"Bah!" yelled Nellie.

Grijpstra, switching into his fatherly mode, was sorry. Nellie, the forgiving darling daughter, forgave Daddy. The warring parties nuzzled.

"My dear," Grijpstra said, remembering the Gerard/de Gier similarity. He always forgot Nellie was allergic to anything to do with Rinus de Gier. "I'm sorry, my dear."

The El Al clerk on the phone asked him to please check in early. Nellie raced the big Bronco to the Amsterdam Airport. She liked to feel the power of the machine, to be high off the ground. She hated having the car filled with gas, waiting at the station, watching numbers flick into an astronomical total. "All this expense is eating up our income."

Grijpstra's defense was that it cost more to ride a wheelchair than a gas guzzler, that expenses could be deducted, that Amsterdam's dangerous lanes and alleys could be best negotiated in a battle car, that he needed the powerful vehicle to impress his clients, like he needed to have Nellie's gable house refurbished to attract good custom.

Nellie took the opportunity to question Grijpstra's monthly trips to Luxembourg.

"I get paid in cash sometimes, dear. The cash goes to a tax-free haven. I go there to invest the money properly."

"And mail monthly checks to Rinus."

"I manage his savings too," Grijpstra admitted.

"So much money you two spend."

Not all that much maybe, and look what it had bought for Nellie: repaired and repainted windowsills, all brick walls filled in and varnished, new copper gutters and drainpipes, the stone angel balancing on the gable's top secured and restored, new oak staircases and floors on all stories, all inside walls whitewashed, beams and posts scraped and oiled, all by the best artisans the city could provide.

"We must be in debt."

"But didn't I refinish the entire basement myself?"

"But why, HenkieLuvvie? I thought you were going to have a heart attack, carrying cement, pouring it yourself. Why didn't you let me help you?"

He had liked refinishing the entire basement himself.

"Just to store all those old files. Those messy cartons."

"A detective needs good files."

"Why did you take your files to Luxembourg?"

"Please." Grijpstra frowned. He had saved. He was making good money now. Not to worry. He sang the Bobby McFerrin line in an attempt at falsetto. "Don't worry. Be happy."

"And your wife, and the kids?"

Mrs. Grijpstra was lady-in-waiting at her rich sister's residence in the country. The kids were grown and all except Ricky on public assistance. If he gave them money they would smoke that too.

"And Ricky at the naval academy?"

Straight A's. A scholarship. Ricky was funded.

Nellie sighed. The El Al ticket, ordered at a moment's notice on his Luxembourg-issued credit card that would need to be paid at the end of the month, had to be expensive too. "You're billing this to Rinus?"

Sure.

"You'll phone me every day?"

You bet.

"But that's costly."

Not if he phoned outside business hours.

"Early mornings?"

Sure.

"But you're never up early mornings."

See you later, dear Nellie.

Chapter 2

Schiphol's departure hall, postmidnight, was empty but for splendidly uniformed military policemen and Israeli agents in jeans and loose jackets. The young woman behind the counter, looking him straight in the eye, wanted to know why Grijpstra insisted on flying El Al. Grijpstra said it: "I'm not Jewish."

He remembered wartime, Grijpstra, Sr., coming home confused after seeing German troops rounding up Jewish citizens on the Dam Square in Amsterdam's center, to transport them to death camps. Grijpstra's dad had been asked for his ID too. He'd said it: "I'm not Jewish."

Was that bad now?

"You said it," the El Al clerk said. "I didn't ask."

"I was reading your mind," Grijpstra said. "I'm a private detective, Ma'am, I sometimes do that. I have a friend in America who is in some trouble. I'm going to help him out."

The clerk checked her screen. "That's why you booked in such a hurry?"

"Yes, ma'am."

"Your friend's trouble?"

"Psychological, ma'am." Grijpstra smiled. "Not to worry. Besides, his grandmother was Jewish."

She smiled too. "What's this *Jewish?*"

"Because you're concerned," Grijpstra said. "You don't want your plane to be blown up, you want to know I'm okay."

"Are you okay?" the clerk asked.

"Oh yes," Grijpstra said.

"So what's your friend's trouble?"

Grijpstra sighed. "Money maybe?"

"He doesn't have money?"

"He has lots and lots of money," Grijpstra said. "He's free of needs. It's hard to be free of needs."

"Your friend is religious?"

"No," Grijpstra said.

"It sometimes helps to keep busy."

"Are you religious?" Grijpstra asked.

"No," the clerk said. "My husband is. He says he's got to be to face the riddle. Do you face the riddle?"

"I'd rather look the other way."

"What if it won't let you?"

"Then it makes me crazy, ma'am."

"Do you have lots and lots of money?"

"Some," Grijpstra said.

"So you're free of needs?"

"Some," Grijpstra said, "but the vacuum doesn't worry me that much. It's beauty that makes me crazy. I try to get it by painting upside-down ducks on canals. I also try to play it on drums."

"Do you ever get it?"

"No," Grijpstra said. He also said that he wasn't carrying any arms or explosives and hadn't accepted any parcels from strangers. She didn't check his luggage.

"You believe me?" Grijpstra asked.

"Some," the clerk said. She smiled.

She looked Egyptian. He thought he'd seen her as a sculpture between hieroglyphics in a museum in Leyden. She had long black hair, an olive skin, very large eyes, and softly carved lips. He asked her. She said her folks had come from Egypt.

The Boeing, rumbling up to the runway, was accompanied by two armored trucks with machine-gun turrets sticking out of their backs. Inside the plane a movie was starting up: Robert Redford in Cuba. Grijpstra watched, listening to music on another channel: Bill Evans on piano, Eddy Gomez on bass. The piano right hand was strong, like a solo horn almost, and the bass—Grijpstra thought that the instrument's bridge had to be moved up to provide such cello-like sounds—answered the piano's questions a little, coming up with questions of its own too, so that the harmo-

nious dialogue might deepen. Robert Redford's tropical
landscape setting was both romantic and fearful, depending
on whether the camera focused on beautiful people on unpolluted beaches or on propeller warplanes strafing beautiful
people on unpolluted beaches. Grijpstra liked the architec-
ture of the Cuban mansions and the sultry actress who
duetted, as Mr. Gomez's bass became her voice here and
there, with Robert Redford, whose pleasing profile took on
sound in the sensitive jazz piano's notes. The attractive actress
could be proud of her country, and she was being very
hospitable, very ready to share.

Grijpstra slept, seeing a sultry Lorraine sharing the
magic of the Maine coast with de Gier, then woke gasping as
she got kicked down a cliff for her troubles.

Chapter 3

       The commissaris, old, wrinkled, small, thin, reflected on his status of *otium cum dignitate*, while watching his knees emerging like twin islands out of the foam of his bubble bath. *Out of office with honor,* so it said, in Latin and gold lettering, on a little mahogany shield handed over by Amsterdam's chief constable when the commissaris, chief of detectives, retired after forty years of representing the queen to serve the people. Katrien, wrapped in a towel, sat on a stool next to the bath and observed her lover. Katrien had her hair in curlers. The commissaris had lost his last hair, except a little fluff on a narrow chest.

       Katrien frowned. "So what are you saying? That de Gier doesn't kick women off cliffs? So what do *you* know? You don't even know the story about the boots and the laces."

       The commissaris's head disappeared at one end of the bath, his foot appeared at the other. The foot moved closer to the faucets. The big toe on the foot adjusted the hot faucet. Toe and foot disappeared. Head reappeared.

"Don't do that," Katrien said. "My father did that. He died. He was having a heart attack. My mother thought he was joking."

The commissaris washed his spectacles and handed them over to Katrien.

"Yes?"

"Please dry them," the commissaris said.

She dried the glasses, leaned over, carefully adjusted the frame across his nose and ears. "Yes?"

"Thank you for drying my glasses," the commissaris said. "I wish you wouldn't wear those curlers, dear."

"Who says you have to look at me? Nellie is right, you know. De Gier shows his true colors now that he's on his own. You could have seen it earlier on but you never wanted to, of course. Just think of the sort of life Rinus was leading."

"Ah." The commissaris smiled.

"Yes," Katrien said. "Too late now, Jan. If I had practiced law, as I wanted to, we could have had an affair. We could have been living apart together. You could have had cats like Oliver and Tabriz and women like what's her name."

"Esther?"

"Can't think of her name now," Katrien said. "Rinus had so many. That motorcycle cop from Friesland, the one who could ride off on one wheel. The long-legged woman."

"Hylkje?"

"Stop licking your chops," Katrien said.

"What sort of law would you have practiced?" the commissaris asked. "Real estate transactions? I think you would have liked that, Katrien. Property attorneys always buy bargains for their own account."

"Yes," she said. "You would have been happier, living alone. Being free, like Rinus. Reading books you don't quite understand. Having me out of the way. Playing that silly mini-trumpet."

"Don't you prefer it to his flute?"

"Yes," Katrien said. "De Gier sounds better on the trumpet. But where does that surrealism get him? Eh? To killing a poor woman?"

"What's with the boots and the laces?" the commissaris asked. "And why be so hard on the boy? You love Rinus, Katrien. You sent him chocolate for Christmas. You make him Indonesian noodles with shrimp crackers when he shows up and I've got to eat it too. You make him stay here so he can mess up my bathroom. You won't leave him alone. You make me jealous. He writes you letters."

"You know what he wrote?" Katrien asked. "That Native Americans call that part of the coast the 'Twilight Zone.' That it's very strange there. That it's the right place to slip away. Away from what, Jan?"

"Away from being a rheumatic in a cold bath," the commissaris said. He struggled to his feet, reaching out to his wife. She caught him as he stepped out of the tub, wrapped him in a towel, rubbed him dry.

"You feel better?"

"Hot water always soaks away some of it," the commissaris said. "The boots and the laces?"

She told him the tale that she had heard from Nellie. Nellie had heard it from Grijpstra ("Nellie Blabbermouth," the commissaris said. "No wonder." "No wonder what, Jan?" "Never mind what, Katrien."), Grijpstra had heard it from de Gier.

Grijpstra and de Gier, both still with the police but about to break free, were spending another evening in their favorite bar, where they could sit in with the house musicians, mostly piano and percussion. They'd been playing "Endless Blues," a composition by de Gier with some interesting dynamics that built carefully from chorus to chorus, and even from section to section within a chorus ("You should write liner notes, Katrien." "You want to hear the rest of this, Jan?" "Yes, Katrien, I'm sorry.") and with some hot scat singing by Grijpstra ("Grijpstra plays drums," the commissaris said. "That means using four limbs already. Now he sings, too?").

Katrien sighed.

They were in the bedroom by now. The commissaris flopped down on the bed, got up, kissed Katrien, lay down again. "Carry on."

"Don't order me around. So Grijpstra sang, and he also did his rising press roll, and the flutter on the side of the snare drum, and the mallet work on bells. He did everything."

"You were there?"

"Of course."

"You never told me."

"I never tell you lots of things," Katrien said. "I was there with Nellie. You were in New York, at the police convention."

"I never go to police conventions."

"Yes," she said. "Please, don't talk rubbish, Jan. Remember that reserve policeman whose uncle immigrated to America and who maybe was murdered in Central Park, and nobody paid attention, and it was his favorite uncle, for the poor fellow had no parents, and he was all upset, being alone in the world now, and asked you to do something. And you said New York was outside your jurisdiction but then that convention came up and you went anyway and found out who did it? With the seeing-eye dog? The dog with the gland trouble? And you had to take care of her too? And the pathologist and the dead girl in the car? With the maggots on her mouth?"

"Yes," the commissaris said. "We all thought it was spittle at first but car trunks get hot. So you were running around town with Nellie?"

"But de Gier was on his own," Katrien said. "He played strangely that night. Like Don Cherry. You know Don Cherry?"

"Yes," the commissaris said. "De Gier likes Don Cherry, that's why he got the mini-trumpet. But de Gier doesn't play that shrilly."

"He's got a softer tone," Katrien said, "but not that

night. He was loud but not bombastic, more like he was in pain. There was a black woman in the bar who picked up on that and she kept singing back to him. They had this dialogue—he was asking and she was giving."

"Words?"

"Just sounds," Katrien said. "She had a beautiful voice, like a bell, like a cymbal too sometimes, you could almost see the sound. Nellie said she could touch it."

"Were you drinking?"

"Nellie brought some pot," Katrien said. "She used to grow it, you know? Out in that courtyard of hers? *Netherweed*. The strongest?

"I would smoke pot," the commissaris said, "just to hear more music from the inside, but I don't want to run around looking for chocolate when all the stores are closed."

"Yes," Katrien said.

"You smoke a lot of pot with Nellie?"

"We decided against it," Katrien said. "Nellie is too easily addicted."

"You're not easily addicted?"

"Remember those codeine pills I got hooked on?" Katrien asked. "Remember the trouble you had to stop smoking?"

"Boots and laces," the commissaris said again. "Let's hear it, Katrien."

"So," Katrien said. "The bar closed, they always do close in the end, and the woman with the bell voice had left, she had someone with her, and Nellie took Grijpstra home and I took a cab and de Gier was alone again, so he went to another bar and another, and to some all-night liquor place and then he got lost."

"Lost?" the commissaris asked.

"In the Red Light District." Katrien pursed her lips. "Your star detective, dead drunk, at four A.M., the light starting up already, birds singing. Your Rinus de Gier tried to have a good time with a prostitute and he had to take his nice new laced boots off, he insisted. And then afterward, after having rolled across the poor woman a few times and been satisfied by artificial means . . ."

"He told you that?" The commissaris gaped.

"He told Grijpstra," Katrien said, "who told Nellie . . ."

"No wonder," the commissaris said.

She snuggled next to him on the bed. "Why do you keep saying 'no wonder,' Jan?"

"What artificial means, Katrien?"

"Some electrical gadget."

The commissaris hissed his surprise. "They have them for men too?"

"Yes, dear. Artificial vaginas. They squeeze and throb. You switch them off afterward and they never argue. You want to hear the rest of this?"

The commissaris grimaced.

"So," Katrien said, "de Gier gets impressed easily, that's why he bought those lace-up boots. He'd seen a movie. The boots were stylish. Wearing them made him think he was

out in the desert fighting Nazis. After he had been relieved
he wanted not only to put his boots on again but to lace them
up too so that he could shoot Field Marshal Rommel in the
Sahara. The woman helped him with one boot but he got
mouthy with her so she put him outside, and then he walked
home, one boot on, one boot off."

"To his apartment?"

"Right."

"From the whore's quarter?"

"Yes, Jan."

"No cabs?"

"He was swaying so badly no cabdriver would risk it."

"Yes," the commissaris said. "They don't like pas-
sengers throwing up on their back seats. Poor de Gier.
Totally out of control. Oh dear."

The commissaris slept badly that night, tossing, turning, mumbling to himself.

"Who is D'Artagnan?" Katrien asked, shaking his
shoulder.

The commissaris had been a musketeer, one of the three
in the French novel; de Gier was D'Artagnan, his pal, but de
Gier had got shot.

"Why are you speaking German?" Katrien asked,
shaking his shoulder again.

The commissaris was replaying a talk show where
elderly German middle-class people, on TV, were asked to
review their lives. They kept saying that, looking back, they

saw nothing but mistakes and calamities; looking ahead they saw only death.

"Please," Katrien said, "stop rubbing your feet. Now what are you doing?"

He mumbled that he was cleaning off dog poop. He'd been walking through the city, barefoot, the last citizen left. All others had fled because Holland's dikes were about to break behind them, due to global warming that melted the polar ice caps. On his way out he kept getting stuck in dog poop. Katrien made hot milk and honey and sprinkled cinnamon on top. She watched him sip.

"Calms the nerves." She patted his cheek. "Feel better now?"

A little later he was mumbling again. "Rinus? I'm coming. Hold on, my boy."

"Go for it, *mon Capitaine*," Katrien whispered.

The commissaris slept well after that, and woke up with a plan. He unfolded his plan.

"Maritime maps of the Maine coast? A tape recorder that connects to a phone?" Katrien asked. "Where do I get those? Connect the gadget to Nellie's phone? Help her to tape her conversations with Grijpstra? Tell her what to ask him? Please . . . where do you think you are? At your office?"

Chapter 4

"Bright and early," Grijpstra said.

El Al had left Amsterdam's Schiphol at 2:00 A.M., flown quietly for five and a half hours, a nice tail wind pushing, and touched down at Boston's Logan at 1:30 A.M.

"Wow," Grijpstra said. He had traveled back in time, he was half an hour younger, he could start part of his life again. If he kept doing this he'd be a baby, still remembering everything, of course. Then what would he do? Be an artist? Stay away from de Gier? Make quite sure he'd never arrive at Boston's Logan at 1:30 A.M. again, with no *one* to take him no*where*?

There was an agent still on duty but she wanted to go home. "I'm sorry, sir, there's no connection to Maine." She checked her screen. "Flights begin at eleven A.M. but they're all booked up for today and tomorrow." She smiled sadly. "It's the season, sir."

"Bus?" Grijpstra asked. "Please?"

She thought there might be one at 8:30 A.M. but it might be full and he'd have to connect to at least one other bus and the total trip might take twelve hours, stop-over time not included.

"Air taxi?" Grijpstra asked. "Please?"

All the numbers the agent dialed played recorded messages that suggested waiting for beeps.

The agent went home.

Grijpstra went to the restroom.

There was another man there, within the vast emptiness of tiled walls and ceilings. The other man did what Grijpstra did—unzip, let go, wait, drip, shake, zip, push faucet, wash hands, push soap button, wash hands, pull towel, rip towel, rub, drop towel into bin.

"Mannequins," the man said. "That's what we are, doing the routine. Like on earth, so in heaven." He looked at Grijpstra. "Don't you think? That this is what heaven's going to be? All this clean space?" He gestured toward the restroom's tiled walls and ceiling. "Sinless?"

Grijpstra was cursing, both his fate and this fellow man, maybe a moron.

"You sick?" the man asked. He looked into Grijpstra's eyes. "You don't look sick. Got something in your throat?" He clapped his hands. "Go on. Cough. Clear it."

"I was swearing," Grijpstra said, "in Dutch."

"You're from Pennsylvania?"

"From where?"

The man and Grijpstra shook clean hands. The man's name was Ishmael. He said he was from the Point in Maine. That'd be in Woodcock County. Grijpstra said he was from Amsterdam. That'd be in Holland. Ishmael said his sister had married a man from there, that'd be in Copenhagen. Where the breakfast buns came from.

"What?" Grijpstra asked.

"The sticky buns," Ishmael said. He knew more, about Danish cheese called Gouda, about Saab cars you could win as prizes that go with magazine subscriptions, about Hans Brinker sticking his finger in the dike.

"Who is Hans Brinker?"

Ishmael said Hans was the Dutch boy you saw on paint labels, and that Hans was also known from textbooks. Finger in hole in dike. Grijpstra thought of Oedipus, desiring his mother, frustrated by his father, therefore, symbolically, sticking his finger in any hole at all. Hans Oedipus?

The name was definitely Brinker, Ishmael said, and Brinker specifically filled holes in Dutch dikes. Ishmael was surprised Grijpstra didn't know his own national hero.

Grijpstra, although willing to please, couldn't place the boy's name.

Ishmael also knew about Holland being a part of Germany. There was World War Two, but he wasn't one to bear grudges, even if a cousin didn't return from the Battle of the Bulge. Too long ago, from the black-and-white days—all that old anger . . . even so, Japan was coming on strong again.

"Holland fought Germany, too," Grijpstra said. "For all of five days."

"Defeat?"

Grijpstra admitted defeat.

"Germany still got you?"

"They gave us back."

"Didn't want to keep you, eh?"

It was all joined into a kind of Europe now, Grijpstra said. They were in it together. That might be better. "Wipe out some borders."

"Like the Canadian border," Ishmael said, "and the Mexican while we're at it. They aren't there anyway. I never see them when I fly across."

"What are the black-and-white days?" Grijpstra asked.

"War documentaries," Ishmael said. "Kind of faded. That's how we saw it then, as little kids. Didn't care much then. No TV, no nothing."

"Ah."

"After Korea it was color."

"To us World War Two was color too," Grijpstra said. Ishmael thought that was amazing.

Ishmael, a small man, wiry, some fifty years old, wearing greenish wide-bottomed cotton trousers and a windbreaker, both well worn and faded, and a duck-billed hat, brand new and bright green, with a weathered face and a set of large very white teeth that he seemed to be holding on to, with his tongue perhaps, or with sucked-in cheeks, was a pilot. As he was bound for home, and the Point was close to Jameson . . .

"I'll pay," Grijpstra said. As in Amsterdam there had been no time to change money, Grijpstra only had Dutch guilders, hundreds, two hundred and fifties and thousands, having grabbed a pile of notes from the basement before leaving. He displayed his wad.

"That's money?" Ishmael asked, looking at the brightly colored notes of different sizes, which showed ornate faces of medieval Dutchmen, stylized flowers, fruit motifs, a bird even, ornamental bands, artistically drawn figures.

"Guilders," Grijpstra said. "One guilder is about half a dollar. There should be plenty here."

"Europe dollars," Ishmael said, shaking his head. "Can't rightly use those in Maine."

Logan Airport was mostly closed inside. The money exchange wouldn't open until 9:00 A.M. There were coffee machines. Ishmael worked one and gave Grijpstra a cup. Grijpstra showed his Diners Club card.

"Ah," Ishmael said. "Can't rightly use that in Maine either. Not where we are at. All empty coast, you know. The bank is a truck, coming in Tuesdays, and it does Visa, but only if you're known, cause there's no phone from the truck, and they only change Canadian dollars, not Europe dollars, I think."

Grijpstra put back his credit card. "I see."

"Bank truck doesn't take pesos either," Ishmael said. "Nothing personal, you know."

"Got to get to Jameson," Grijpstra said. He explained about his friend watching nature out there from an island, Squid Island.

"That's next to Bar Island," Ishmael said. "I fly around there some. Bar Island has this bar that connects to the peninsula of Jameson that gets submerged at low tide."

"Jameson goes under water?"

"No, just the bar to Bar Island." Ishmael's teeth clicked as he laughed. "Jameson too, when this ozone hole opens up a bit more. That hole is right above the coast of Maine, did you know that? That'll warm us up all right. What do you do for a living?"

Grijpstra explained that he was a former cop, now a private detective.

"Your friend on Squid Island, would he be a cop too?"

That was amazing, Ishmael said, two former European cops watching nature on three thousand miles of Maine coast (counting all the nooks and crannies) not too well guarded by the Coast Guard, the Marine Patrol, sheriffs' offices, justice departments, the DEA, the what-have-you.

"DEA?"

"Drug Enforcement Agency," Ishmael said.

"You got drugs in Maine?"

Ishmael's teeth were clicking again. "You got drugs in Dutchland?"

Grijpstra said he didn't care about drugs. He thought

that over three thousand miles of not-too-well-guarded coast might attract some, though.

"So," Ishmael said, "you're in a hurry to start watching some nature with your former cop friend out on Squid Island. Now if you rented a car, you'd be there in ten hours."

"I'd rather fly with you," Grijpstra said. "I could pay you later."

"You could," Ishmael said. He didn't like to fly in the dark, though, so they'd have to wait for daybreak, three hours away. Grijpstra slept in the lounge, waking up every now and then to listen to Ishmael snore in the seat next to him, or to accept more coffee or candy bars that Ishmael kept getting from machines.

The plane was small, red and white, and had double wings, covered with what, to Grijpstra, appeared to be sailcloth. It was tied to the tarmac with ropes. Grijpstra helped undo them. There was only a small bench inside, with a little space behind it that Grijpstra's bag fitted into. Ishmael's bag balanced on top. The dashboard wasn't too complicated.

"1949," Ishmael said. "A Tailorcraft. They don't build them now. You okay there?"

Grijpstra was too big maybe but he didn't say so. He watched Ishmael turn the wooden propeller and listened to the little engine ahead, sputtering before catching. Ishmael hoisted himself up, patted the dashboard, took out a portable radio, and called the control tower. The Tailorcraft began to spin as it reached the runway.

"Hello?" Ishmael asked the plane. "Would you mind? Oh, I see."

It was Grijpstra's right foot, depressing the plane's right wheel brake. The plane had double everything.

"Don't touch nothing," Ishmael said. The plane finished its full turn and tried again. Ishmael was wearing little headphones connected to his portable radio. Control must have told him to go, for the plane took off, suddenly and bravely, into an empty sky that connected, Grijpstra reflected, to the rest of the universe, which was nothing really, a void, without coordinates except the lines that man had come up with.

"Nothing," Grijpstra shouted over the engine's puny roar.

"What?" Ishmael shouted.

"Even less than your heaven," Grijpstra said, pointing ahead and to the sides, even to the rear, where, turning his head with some difficulty, he could see only the plane's toy tail, sticking up comically between two little white clouds suspended in an infinity of blues, in assorted shades, all transparent.

"Heaven?"

"Your restroom heaven."

Ishmael shouted that he'd been dreaming about heaven before meeting Grijpstra. The Tailorcraft, flying horizontally now above the Massachusetts coast line, replaced its tiny roar with a quiet putt-putt. "Maybe you're the angel," Ishmael said. "There should be angels in heaven, but in my dream, there was only the restroom and a uniformed guy shining shoes, a black, white-haired guy, he was Saint Peter, his nameplate said so, he wanted to know what I'd been doing."

"In charge of thresholds," Grijpstra said.

"That's him." Ishmael rolled a cigarette with one hand, out of a can from the glove compartment. There was a soldier on the can blowing a trumpet. "You want one?"

Grijpstra didn't.

"They still smoke in Holland?"

"Oh yes," Grijpstra said, reassured by the Boston suburbs below, crawling up along the coast in repetitive patterns. There were sailboats too, and ferries, busily connecting clearly visible points A and B. He'd probably be fine, sitting on the plane's sailcloth wings, waving and screaming. Social suburbanites, sunning their worked-out bodies on their balconies, would pick up a phone, or old salts, ferry captains, weathered pleasure sailors, would turn a wheel. Not to worry.

"They don't smoke here no more," Ishmael said. "Just me and Hairy Harry occasionally. Looks funny, puffy rosy cheeks and then that fat cigar. Where was I, Krip?"

Grijpstra thought they were flying out of Where, if there were a Where anywhere now that they were out of coordinates below—no houses, no boats.

"The dream." Ishmael blew thick smoke at the plane's cracked windscreen. "Saint Peter wanted to know who-what-where and I said I had been this Maine Pentecostal person. You know? Pentecost? Whitsunday? Holy Ghost coming down? You don't cut your hair much and the women wear long dresses and you go to chapel most of the time?"

"Right," Grijpstra said happily. The shoreline had showed up again: some houses, a sizable boat.

"You got the Holy Ghost coming down Whitsunday at your end too?"

"Yes," Grijpstra said. There was an Uncle Joe who lived in the country, Holland's religious part, where kids weren't vaccinated against polio and everybody put out the flag on the queen's birthday. Uncle Joe was a healer.

"Ever heal anybody?"

Not to Grijpstra's knowledge but Uncle Joe did speak in tongues.

"Like you," Ishmael said, "in the restroom. Okay. So I told Saint Peter I had been doing that, and more, praying extra hours, going to chapel before breakfast, preaching, hollering and whatnot, guiding the congregation, rolling about the floor speaking in tongues, and he said, 'Very well, sir, that'll be the second door on the right then.'"

The houses below were getting further apart and there was only one ship, a huge tanker, the size of some of the bigger islands they had passed earlier, that appeared to move just a little slower, it seemed to Grijpstra, than the Tailor-craft. Grijpstra remembered a yachtsman in Holland who washed up on the beach after his craft got torn up by a gale. The yachtsman told a TV interviewer he'd been floating on top of big waves and there were tankers everywhere and when the yachtsman looked into the tankers' portholes he kept seeing sailors enjoying their dinners, or watching TV, or un-centerfolding *Playboys,* and nobody saw him outside, begging and sobbing.

"Second door on the right," Ishmael repeated, "and we're in the airport restroom, so that door would lead into one of the shitters. But that's where he said I had to go and he was Saint Peter—he had a label on his chest that said so."

Grijpstra groaned.

"Bad," Ishmael said, "but I'm from Maine so I don't believe nothing unless my parents tell me to and my parents are dead. So I just stand about for a bit and there's other people having their shoes shined and they never did the Pentecost and you know where Saint Peter sent them?"

"No," Grijpstra said. He thought he shouldn't worry because this Tailorcraft had been around since 1949, with good people like Ishmael at the controls. Nothing to fear but fear itself. And say, just for argument's sake, that the plane did go down. This was not a good planet anyway. This might even be hell. To leave could only be pleasant. Nellie was okay perhaps but no more memory of the significant person in one's life means no more regret at being without that significant person. What else would death wipe out? Amsterdam traffic? Old age? Traveling in old unreliable mini-airplanes? More and more red tide in the sea and a lot of people being kept alive with terminal painful diseases? He should be grateful. Here he was having the last bad time of his bad life.

"Second door on the right," Ishmael said. "All of them.

All of them got sent through the second door on the right. One total asshole I knew, he'd lived in a commune—Zen, you know Zen?"

"My friend does," Grijpstra said, looking straight ahead. "My friend Rinus, on Squid Island. Back in Amsterdam he'd go sometimes, Sunday mornings. Said he would sit on thin cushions, his legs all twisted, quietly, never mind if it hurt."

"On Squid Island?"

"No, in a loft, in Amsterdam. *Lange Leidse Dwarsstraat honderd drie en veertig drie hoog.*"

"You're okay?" Ishmael asked.

"I'm sorry," Grijpstra said. "I thought you wanted to know where Rinus did Zen. That was the address."

"In tongues?"

"In Dutch."

"What happens to Rinus when he does Zen?"

"When he stops sitting his legs stop hurting. So where did your Zen man get sent by Saint Peter?

"Second door on the right," Ishmael said. "Like everybody else. Never mind what he'd done. Maybe played golf and fished for trout all his life. Maybe nine to fived for IBM or Ford. Watched daytime TV. Same difference—all us suckers. But there were all the other doors too—those are big restrooms at Logan, fifty doors maybe—so I wondered where they led to. And there were all these folks getting their shoes shined by Peter, keeping the old boy busy so that he couldn't see what was going on behind him. So I sneaked around, tried all the other doors, and you know what?"

"Duds," Grijpstra said. "Dud doors. Part of the wall between Now and Hereafter. Only the second door worked."

"You had the same dream?"

"Makes sense," Grijpstra said. "Doesn't it? You tried the second door?"

"Sure," Ishmael said. "Led to Bliss. More of the same with the pain blocked out. Whatever you wanted to do you could do. All the shoe-shined people were there, looking for something to do. But I wanted to make music and there were these black guys who said they would let me play with them so I was going to do that for a while but they said it wouldn't satisfy me forever."

"Yes," Grijpstra said.

"You had the same dream?"

"What's your instrument?" Grijpstra asked.

"Keyboards." Ishmael had been rolling more cigarettes out of the trumpeting-soldier can and he had to crack a window to let air into the cockpit. There was too much wind whistling in to talk through but Ishmael pointed things out below, with the coast roughening up. No more townhouses on sand beaches raked by tractors but bays, coves, peninsulas, and ragged islands, each with its own moving luminous froth surrounding bare rocks leading up to carpets of shrubs and firs or pine trees. There were a few fishing boats thumping through turbulent seas, white wooden vessels, and a three-masted schooner with billowing brown sails.

"Tourist charter boat," Ishmael shouted.

There was a modern yacht, sleek, whizzing along under a cloud of white nylon. Grijpstra thought that the yacht was the ideal situation.

Ishmael made the plane lose altitude. The Tailorcraft, its tiny wheels a few feet above the waves, circled the yacht. The crew waved. The crew looked young and beautiful, both sexes from late teens to thirties. Grijpstra thought that these had to be the Magazine Cover People, temporarily released from their second dimension. He noticed a white-maned, ruddy-faced, sharp-featured, tall military-looking authority at the wheel. The authority smoked a pipe. Grijpstra thought the authority could be General MacArthur, or the United States god. Grijpstra waved. General MacArthur or the United States god lifted an imperial hand in response. There was immense power in the figure.

The little plane headed north again. Grijpstra thought of de Gier, subject to American authority now. "Do you know Sheriff Hairy Harry?"

Ishmael discussed Hairy Harry while the Tailorcraft wiggled through the last hundred miles to Jameson, in between showing his passenger such curiosities as a finback whale coming up to spout between dives, over seventy feet of smoothly shaped gray-blue creature calmly pursuing a majestic existence framed by whitecaps on green waves.

"Thirty elephants," Ishmael said, "thirty elephants wouldn't outweigh that mother."

"Big mother," Grijpstra said, as the whale dwarfed the airplane.

"Bigger than Tyrannosaurus rex," Ishmael said, "and that mother stood five stories. What did you hear about our sheriff?"

"To stay away?" Grijpstra asked.

Ishmael thought that might be a good idea. Grijpstra might think this whale was big but Sheriff Hairy Harry was bigger. Why, did Grijpstra know that Hairy Harry, ruler of Woodcock County, Maine, had bought a two-hundred-thousand-dollar house from Farnsworth for one hundred thousand, twenty-five down, and an easy mortgage?

"From Flash Farnsworth?" Grijpstra asked.

"So you know everybody?" Ishmael's dentures clicked in amazement, moved sideways a little, overadjusted, came back in place. "No. *Bildah* Farnsworth. He'd be kin to Flash. All Flash has is an osprey nest for hair and a half share in a leaky tub."

Grijpstra said there had to be a slump on for houses to sell at half their value, and Ishmael said that would be so, but then there was always a recession in Maine. But Hairy Harry's house was custom-built, complete—turn the key and step into Hairy Harry Land, the sheriff's individually adjusted theme park. Country music on compact disc in an electronic jukebox loudspeaker-extended to all rooms, full-size snooker tables in the basement, inside golf carpet wall to wall in the loft, bar with foreign beers on tap, a gun room, a video room.

Ishmael looked sly. Now he wasn't sure but just for the sake of argument, of pure cussedness, there might even be a supply of skinflicks there, no kidding around for Hairy Harry, the old in-and-out perhaps. Imported, most likely. Probably quite a collection. Ishmael liked to collect things himself and there was something to be said for naked women, okay? Grijpstra didn't mind his bringing up the subject? But they, the women, might make the viewer, Ishmael in this case, kind of nervous, especially if they moved and talked, and had company and so forth. "You happen to care for that sort of thing yourself, eh . . ."

"Grijpstra."

"Kripstra," Ishmael said.

"In Holland we get too much of that now," Grijpstra said. "Like masturbation classes on prime-time TV. Holland used to be Calvinistic all over but it's the other way around now. The Dutch are compulsive in any direction. Prescribed group sex and all that." Grijpstra didn't care for the activity himself.

"What if they're good?"

Grijpstra said he always preferred them to be out of sight, behind drawn curtains. "And quiet," Grijpstra said. "They better be quiet."

"You could switch them off."

Grijpstra said his girlfriend liked to watch sometimes.

"You really don't like looking in?"

"Makes me shy," Grijpstra said.

"That's like Flash Farnsworth," Ishmael said. "Flash closes his eyes at the good parts."

"Porno?"

"No, regular," Ishmael said. "But regular shows it too. Flash says he can see it better in his head."

"Flash with the bird's nest on top?"

"Right." Ishmael made the Tailorcraft skim waves, nip between islands here and there, while he told Grijpstra about Flash, and while summer people, lounging on verandas of island summer houses, looked down on the antique airplane putt-putting bravely below.

Flash Farnsworth, Ishmael remembered, was with the Coast Guard once, and a drinking lad at the time, until divine justice sent the big woman bouncing down the boulevard in Boston. So now Flash limped. "You see, Krip, that's what Flash finally figured out the big woman to be—heaven-sent. Get me?"

Amsterdam police officers, in view of the city's partly alien population, are required to take English spoken-language exams. Grijpstra also watched American rental movies, with Tabriz, de Gier's left-behind fat furry cat, bunched up on his lap, blocking the subtitles. On the other hand there were Ishmael's Maine accent and Grijpstra's fear of flying low in a small aircraft above turbulent seas. Nevertheless Grijpstra got the general drift of Flash's trial, which, Ishmael said, had to do with faith and reason, and the simplicity of Flash, who wanted God in heaven. One who accepts nothing at all, Ishmael said, has to look for reasons to hang his soul from.

"Always for a reason," Ishmael was saying. "Got to be the Lord who sent this woman. So here is Flash, marching along on the Boston boulevard, with a flask in his back pocket, in his Sunday whites, and there's Bigga, bouncing along, and divine design says they gotta meet, right, Krip?"

Grijpstra nodded, wondering about the splashing against the windscreen. What was it, sea spray? Had to be spray, with the plane flying that low.

"So Bigga wants the flask and Flash wants Bigga and divine design provides the side street and the alley off the side street and a garbage can in the alley, and Bigga puts Flash on the lid and sets herself down on him and . . ."

Ishmael's two-tone whistle and the flat of his hand hitting his thigh rhythmically indicated their having sex.

"Flash is a quiet man, but at that particular time and place Flash was yelling, and Bigga thought that it was she who caused this joyful agony, but it was the broken flask up Flash's ass." Ishmael sang:

And all the Coast Guard's surgeons
and all the Navy's men
couldn't put Flash's rear end
together again.

Grijpstra wished he had never taken the English courses, never watched the American rentals. Full comprehension of Flash's anal problem turned his testicles to glass.

JANWILLEM VAN DE WETERING

He concentrated on the windscreen, with moisture splashing up, dribbling back to the hood. Ishmael had made the plane fly high again, at some five hundred feet, veering back to the coast. The weather was good: clear sky with thin cloud lines parallel to the horizon.

"What's that fluid on the windscreen?" Grijpstra finally asked.

Ishmael, still discussing the human necessity to make sense of things, even of Bigga on Boston Common, and the human refusal to allow for random occurrence, switched his window wipers on.

"It isn't raining," Grijpstra said.

The fluid was gasoline. Ishmael wasn't surprised. This had happened before. "You see, Kripstra, there's an old gas tank in the port wing and another in the starboard wing and the gas pump sucks in rust that clogs the tube to the engine and the pump keeps pumping so the tube bursts a bit."

"So now the gas runs on top of the engine and not into the engine?" Grijpstra asked.

The engine spluttered.

Grijpstra reflected on whether ending equals beginning. Is death birth?

"The engine's still trying." Ishmael checked the dashboard. "For a while." He patted his passenger's hand. "You're right, we don't want high-octane gasoline, the world's most popular explosive, run on top of a hot engine, do we, Krip?"

"We do not," Grijpstra said.

The hills of Jameson were in sight. So was the town

itself, a crescent of pastel-colored Victorian mansions, with a second tier of more modest frame houses, mostly plain white, rectangular, for more regular folks. A few of the larger frame houses carried cupolas, little watchtowers, offering sea views. There were thin-spired churches. The bigger church showed the creator's giant eye on its front wall, sea blue, with long lashes, looking benevolently at the approaching airplane.

Grijpstra only saw the hills with granite slopes, thinly overgrown by spruces, or just bare, glaring, harsh, waiting for the little plane to smash into them.

"Jameson airstrip is on the other side of the hills there," Ishmael said, cutting the engine. "Can't make that, I think, not unless we want to catch fire. Let's aim for the critters, shall we?"

The critters were sheep, running about nervously as the Tailorcraft, aimed at their meadow, lost height rapidly.

The little plane was gliding quietly down, taking its time, giving Grijpstra a chance to check out the harbor, where Jameson's small fleet of lobster vessels had attached themselves to moorings, between ledges dotted with sea gulls and cormorants. Grijpstra saw a string of islands, one squidshaped, with a short body and numerous tentacles of dotted rock lines fanning outward. A peninsula reached into the sea from Jameson, bending toward the islands, of which the first, semi-attached with a bar of glistening wet sand and ledge, was clearly visible through what could be some ten feet of pale green water. He saw shoals of shiny fish, and cormorants, wings stretched, twisting and diving in pursuit.

Grijpstra took in the beauty of the scene below, in spite of, or perhaps because of, being scared, the fear that sharpens perception.

The plane landed, hopping about on clumps of grass, following the galloping sheep, twisting and turning.

"It'll be your foot on the brake again," Ishmael said. Grijpstra pulled back his legs. The Tailorcraft, about to fall over, righted itself neatly.

A large four-wheel drive came trundling up a dirt road, blue lights quietly flashing, then stopped at the fence. The vehicle was marked SHERIFF. Hairy Harry jumped out nimbly. The sheep's leader, a mighty ram with curled horns, left his flock to confront the intruder. The sheriff, turning back from replacing the field's wooden gate, put his hand on his gun.

Ishmael came running. "Now, now," Ishmael said, maneuvering between beast and man, "none of that, Harry."

The sheriff put the revolver away. "Rams scare me, Ishy." He spoke in a high childlike voice that matched his hairless head. A naked head, Grijpstra thought. Hairy Harry was still explaining. "We had a ram on the farm. I'd have to take a jug of cold coffee out to my dad and the ram would run me down. I'd spill the coffee, my dad would beat on me." Hairy Harry smiled widely, showing good teeth, which he shouldn't have, Grijpstra thought, being that hairless and babylike. "You hear what I'm trying to tell you, Ishy?"

"I hear you," Ishmael said, scratching the ram between his horns. "It's okay now, Harry."

The sheriff kept his smile. "Saw you both come tootlin' down, thought I'd check you out, Ishy." Harry pushed up the rim of a new-looking straw hat. "Was expecting you two in a way. Tad of trouble?"

Ishmael mentioned rusty gas tubes and a persistent fuel pump. He walked the ram back to his sheep. "Sorry about using the common. This here is Kripstra, Sheriff."

"Let's see what we have here," the sheriff said after shaking hands. "Wouldn't be bringing in anything from away, would we? Anything we wouldn't need here? Mind if I frisk you? Could you turn around, sir?"

Grijpstra was patted down and asked to produce the contents of his pockets. The sheriff checked the wallet, studying an ID card with a photograph and the red, white, and blue colors of the Dutch flag. "Detective?"

"Private," Grijpstra said.

"Mr. Marlowe," Hairy Harry said, "Mr. Foreign Marlowe. You read Chandler, Krip? I'm a Charles Willeford man myself but Willeford's guy is a cop. Always wanted to meet with a private eye, though. Not too many of your kind around here, Krip." He pulled a thousand-guilder note from Grijpstra's wallet. "How much in dollars?"

"Five hundred," Grijpstra said, "maybe a little over now."

The sheriff counted the wad. "Twenty-two thousand guilders makes eleven thousand dollars?"

"Right," Grijpstra said.

"You carrying that much cash for a reason?"

"For the trip," Grijpstra said. "It came up in a hurry. I thought I might need some."

Hairy Harry returned the wallet. "That'll be all for now, sir. You'd have a purpose for your visit? Business? Pleasure?"

Ishmael frowned. "You'd know that, Harry, from listening in on the open CB channel. You knew Rinus asked me to pick up a friend at Logan Airport. This is a free country, Harry."

"Oh yes." Harry held his smile, keeping his message serious in its wording only. "Free not to bother well-meaning local folks going about their customary business, is that what you mean?"

A jeep pulled up at the other side of the sheep fence and a uniformed deputy got out—a younger man, tall, military looking. The deputy saluted the sheriff and nodded at Ishmael.

"This is Kripstra, Deputy Billy Boy," Ishmael said.

"How're you doing, Kripstra." There was no question mark.

Grijpstra said he was doing good anyway. Nice place, this Jameson.

While Billy helped the sheriff to check the airplane and Ishmael's and Grijpstra's bags, Grijpstra walked over to the Bronco. He was admiring the car's steel running boards when the sheriff joined him.

"Like 'em, Kripstra?"

Grijpstra said he certainly did, he would like to equip his own Ford with running boards like that.

"You drive an American vehicle, Kripstra?"

Grijpstra said he did.

"They still have American vehicles over in Europe? Between them Toyotas and such?"

They sure had.

Grijpstra became enthusiastic. He told Hairy Harry that Holland had been liberated by Americans and Canadians and the British. Poles too, a Polish regiment came from England. But it was the Americans who impressed young Grijpstra, standing on Dam Square in Amsterdam, clutching his mother's hand.

"Those are Yanks, HenkieLuvvie."

The Yanks were in a tank looking down, chewing gum, grinning at little Grijpstra, who was waving his piece of orange cloth attached to a dowel—orange stood for the House of Orange, for the queen, for goodness, for the loving mother who'd come back to her country to rule it in peace, thanks to Yanks chewing gum in tank turrets.

"So you're all still white Protestants out there in liberated Holland," said Billy, "and now you're joining your pal Rinus on Squid Island. What would that be for?"

"To watch nature," Grijpstra said.

"No kidding?"

"Holland's getting too full," Grijpstra said. He told the sheriff and deputy what Katrien had been telling him, last

JANWILLEM VAN DE WETERING

time he called on the ailing commissaris to pay his respects. Katrien quoted recently published statistics. "Nine hundred Dutchmen to the square mile, nine hundred pigs to the same square mile, twenty-three cows to the same square mile, twenty-three cars to the same square mile."

"How big a country are we talking about, Kripstra?"

Grijpstra was still working on how much three hundred kilometers times a hundred kilometers, less allowing for a skinny waist and one southern leg reaching down, would come to in United States measurements when Ishmael helped out. Holland, said Ishmael, which he hadn't believed was there—who could believe Squid Island's Rinus?—had turned up in Ishmael's encyclopaedia and was half the size of Maine. The sixteen million Dutchmen were also likely to exist. Ishmael's old *Encyclopaedia Britannica* only listed five million of the creatures, but that was in 1890 and didn't the human affliction keep multiplying all the time thanks to medical science? And sixteen million Dutchmen spread out in half the state of Maine, why, that would equal out at around nine hundred a square mile, as the man was saying. "That's a lot of crawling around in a space the size of Jameson, don't you reckon?"

The sheriff said he liked people fine but people tended to exaggerate at times. He said Billy Boy was a great man for numbers. Hairy Harry asked Billy Boy to confirm Ishmael's statement.

"That could be right, Hairy Harry."

"How many of us in Maine now, Billy Boy?"

"About a million, Hairy Harry."

"Sixteen million customers," the sheriff said, "crawling all over each other, and you were in the police a good while, tending to their crawling, isn't that right, Kripstra?"

Grijpstra said he had had that pleasure until two years ago.

"And now you're watching nature, you and the other retiree cop? What else'd you be watching?"

"Just nature," Grijpstra said.

Hairy Harry apologized for any inconvenience he might have caused. He leaned out of his car window.

"Good watching, Krip. We'll be watching your watching."

Chapter 5

Billy drove Ishmael and Grijpstra to Beth's Diner for a late breakfast. It was ten o'clock by then, but Billy Boy and Ishmael said that, as the lobster boats were coming in from early-morning trap lifting, the restaurant would be jumping. Grijpstra remembered his lack of dollars.

"Rinus will have some," Ishmael said, "you could call him."

"No phone on Squid Island," Grijpstra said.

Billy Boy pulled a microphone from under the jeep's dashboard. "This is America, Krip. Everything works." He pushed the microphone's button. "Squid Island, this is your sheriff. Come in, Rinus."

The radio produced a little static.

"Must be out of the house," Ishmael said, "or he could be coming into town on the *Kathy Three*." Billy Boy pushed his button. "*Kathy Three,* this is your sheriff, come in, *Kathy Three.*"

The radio produced more static.

"Flash and Bad George don't worry much," Ishmael said. "They're also hard of hearing. Their diesel might be thumping too."

Grijpstra moaned.

"You hungry?"

Grijpstra had gained weight since leaving the force. He now liked to keep it up, to project an image of the heavy detective, the man of substance. Nellie helped: her cooking was designed to keep her men stout.

"De Gier could be in the diner," Ishmael said. "If he isn't, he might be coming."

Grijpstra noticed Akiapola'au after he'd eaten the stacked pancakes with whipped butter, the home fries with parsley, the extra large eggs over easy, the little steak to the side with the choice of sauces, the pumpernickel toast, the fresh orange juice.

"More coffee?"

"Oh yes, miss."

"I'm Akiapola'au, you can call me Aki."

Aki said she was from Hawaii, the big island, Kona Coast. Had he ever been there, seen the volcano boil and the little finches eat dead flesh?

Grijpstra burped politely behind his hand, saying,

"Excuse me." He hadn't been to Hawaii, or anywhere really, he'd only been to Antwerp to eat mussels. Antwerp was just down the street from Holland, in Belgium, a few hours' drive, well worth the effort to eat mussels, but he wouldn't care to go further, and he wouldn't be here in America on the other side of the globe if his good friend Rinus hadn't insisted—so now where *was* Rinus?

Grijpstra liked talking to Aki, who seemed fascinated by his accent. She was tall and lovely, exotic, black hair down to wide shoulders, doe-eyed, dressed in silk under her little apron—a tight skirt cut up along the thighs so that she could move around easily, her blouse low cut. "Nicely stacked," Grijpstra thought.

"We've got mussels here," Aki said. "The locals think they're trash food, but they're good. My Beth could steam some."

"Your Beth," Grijpstra said.

Aki smiled. "Beth and I are a couple. She steams mussels with jalapeños—my own crop, I grow them in planters."

She had to go, there were mouths to feed, bearded mouths of bulky rough-looking men in yellow plastic coats, tall boots, turtleneck sweaters, flat hats with black braid on the visors.

"It's cold on the water," Ishmael said, "always some ten degrees below what it is here on land, twenty at times. And it gets chilly on land; there's no Gulf Stream here like you have in Europe."

"So Rinus sent you to pick me up in Boston?" Grijpstra asked.

Ishmael smiled. "You didn't know, Detective?"

Grijpstra sipped coffee.

"A plane out of Woodcock County, Maine?" Ishmael asked. "Lots of counties in Maine." Ishmael squinted. "A coincidence? Me piddling next to you in an empty airport? Lots of restrooms in Logan Airport. Two coincidences too many maybe, Detective?"

Grijpstra smiled, to show appreciation of Ishmael's humor. "So you do fly at night. You'd just arrived at Logan in the dark. You needed some time to rest. Is that why we waited?"

"You knew or you didn't?" Ishmael said.

"So how do I get to Squid Island?" Grijpstra asked. "You can't fly me there, and the *Kathy Three* isn't responding. Shall I row?"

"You could get Aki to drive you to the Point," Ishmael said. "There'll be dories there, but you've got to watch out for the tide. It's low now, and low tide tends to pull you out to the ocean."

Ishmael had to tend to his airplane. "Don't get stuck on the sand flats, Kripstra." Ishmael put money on the check that Aki had left on the table, shook hands with Grijpstra, said they'd meet again. "Enjoy your stay, Krip. Take care."

Grijpstra didn't get that. Too much was happening. There was Jameson Harbor outside, apparently known as 'the Point,' where rowboats were kept and where Ishmael seemed to live. Grijpstra got up and looked out of a window. The harbor didn't appear pointed at all. And it was close. Why would Aki have to drive him to a nearby harbor? There were fishing boats tugging at their moorings and a good-size new-looking yacht, similar to the other expensive sailboat with the divine captain and his timeless crew that Grijpstra had seen from Ishmael's airplane. This yacht was tied down with a frayed-looking anchor cable that was yanking her sleek bow down sharply. Grijpstra read the yacht's name on the stern, in elegant white italics on varnished teak: *Macho Bandido*. He also saw a row of dories, obviously used to row fishermen to their boats. The dories were tied up to the quayside. He could maybe borrow one. He looked at the garland of islands at the end of the bay beyond the harbor. The tide would be out, baring sand banks that he could see stretching out behind markers. Squid Island must be beyond the sand banks. If his rowboat got stuck he would have to wait for high tide to come in and float him and then he'd have to row against the tide. Better be careful now. Wind direction? He checked the way the waves were rolling. Away from the harbor. Very nice. No big deal. Up. And away.

Aki came by to pick up Ishmael's money. "More coffee, dear?"

He watched the slender hand tipping the pot. He thanked Aki.

Now, Grijpstra thought, there was a given set of circumstances here, and there was his intelligent self, and there had to be a way his intelligent self could manipulate those circumstances optimally. De Gier should be here to help but de Gier's absence, alas, proved his assholery. Grijpstra didn't want to think that way about a fellow musician he played "Endless Blues" with, practicing what had been called, by a slumming journalist writing about amateur jazz, a "loose irresistible shuffle beat," he didn't want to classify a colleague as such, a brother policeman he had shared a working life-time with, twenty years of watching the city of Amsterdam getting steadily worse, from an unmarked rustbucket Volks-wagen mostly, with no springs, ever-steamed-up windows and a radio that crackled in between directing its hapless crew to scenes of domestic violence: "Did your husband beat you, ma'am? "No, I fell." "Did your wife blacken your eye, sir?" "No, it's always black." "So who phoned for assistance, ma'am?" "The goddamn neighbors."

Where was asshole de Gier? Safely tucked away while his savior crossed an ocean in an airplane that had to be protected from terrorists by armored vehicles with machine guns on top, and while his guardian angel flew in a kite soaked in explosives, and while his redeemer was abused by authorities. . . . Was he really expected to row across an ocean to an island?

Grijpstra would rather be ferried. He smiled at the woman behind the counter, loading more plates. "You must be Beth. I'm Kripstra, guest of Rinus de Gier."

Beth smiled too. She had cascading chins and bulging arms and breasts like stuffed hammocks. She had large blue eyes. The eyes were very clear. "Pleased to meet you. Coming to watch nature too?"

Grijpstra kept smiling. He explained his presence. He painted ducks on Sunday afternoons, upside-down ducks, using their orange feet for little sails. Nature always turned him on. "Yes, ma'am." Nature. Nature Woman. Dead nature woman Lorraine, floating upside down in that vast ocean out there?

Facing the younger woman he was being friendly-fatherly, he was good at that. When he and de Gier policed Amsterdam's inner city, de Gier bothered the suspect while Grijpstra took care, held hands, bought coffee, worried about his client's feelings, read him his rights.

Grijpstra smiled.

He spotted a gray metal box on the shelf behind the counter. There was a microphone connected to the box.

"Is that your CB radio? You think you could reach the *Kathy Three?*"

Grijpstra remembered the commissaris summing up his New World experience. "Americans mean well. If they can figure out what it is you want them to help you out with, and they think they can help you out, they will."

"Sure." Beth activated her set. "*Kathy Three,* this is Beth, come in, *Kathy Three.*"

The radio crackled.

Beth tried Squid Island too. "Rinus, this is Beth . . ."

Beth shook her head. "Nothin' doin'."

"I could row, couldn't I?"

"Sure," Beth said. If he'd wait a moment she'd take him to the Point, or Aki could take him, but there were still too many fishermen in the restaurant. Would he mind waiting? Could she get him more coffee? "Excuse me, Kripstra." New customers had come in. "Seat yourselves, dears."

Grijpstra wandered away from the counter. He knew where the rowboats were and he could see Squid Island. He'd left his bag at the table. Aki handed it to him. He liked Aki. Aki and Beth, was it? Nellie had gay friends too. She was probably bisexual. He had never dared to ask.

At the quay Grijpstra met Little Max, son of Big Max the lobsterman. Little Max was fishing from his dad's dory.

"Hi."

Little Max said hi too.

They exchanged names.

"My friend Rinus lives on Squid Island, Little Max. I'm going to stay with him for a while. I'd like to row out there. Can I borrow your dory? I'll bring it back when the tide turns and then I'll pay you ten dollars."

"Ten dollars," Little Max said thoughtfully.

Grijpstra, to diminish distance—he was good with dogs too—sat on his haunches. "You know the man out on Squid Island, the fellow who watches nature? You must have seen the foreign man. I wanted to go with the *Kathy Three*, with Flash Farnsworth? And Bad George? But Beth can't raise them on the CB, so now I'll have to row."

Little Max was impressed. This outsider sure knew names. Grijpstra had shaved on the El Al airplane, and his worsted suit didn't look too crumpled. The leather bag was new. Little Max thought this knowledgeable fellow, talking "from away," sure looked like a banker. Little Max had seen Bostonian bankers before, they came out to fish or hunt and they spread dollars around like crazy but so far not to him. Ten big ones' worth of Beth's chocolate-chip ice cream; he could spread that out some.

Grijpstra rowed. He hadn't lost his touch since his father had taken him out fishing some forty years ago. The oars stayed in their locks, little waves broke musically against the bow behind him. His direction was good for he'd drawn a line between Squid Island behind his back and Jameson's tallest church spire facing him now and if he could just manage to keep that spire between his feet, which were planted firmly against the dory's rear seat, and look over his shoulder once in while to check out the other end, he should make it easily, he thought. The tide pulled and the wind pushed, a breeze that kept strengthening as the dory got further out of Jameson. The waves increased in size. He saw a beige-colored speedboat leaving Jameson Harbor, powered by twin outboards. It approached rapidly. As the speedboat skipped across waves, wavering a bit before coming back on course, Grijpstra could read the lettering on both sides of the bow: SHERIFF'S DEPARTMENT WOODCOCK COUNTY. The boat was fair-sized, thirty feet long at least, sleek, dangerous, and efficient. A shark prowling.

Hairy Harry was at the console, standing behind the

wheel. Billy Boy, protected by curved glass, crouched in the bow. The sheriff smiled, Billy Boy didn't. "How're you doing?"

"Good," Grijpstra said.

The outboards, in neutral, growled mightily. The powerboat stopped next to the dory. "We're enforcing rules today," Billy Boy said. "You been studying sea rules, Krip?"

"Not lately," Grijpstra said.

Billy had a checklist, clipped to a board. He also had a ballpoint. He was ready to make some checkmarks.

"Life jacket?"

"No life jacket."

"Horn?"

"No horn."

No bail bucket either. No extra paddle. No flashlight. No flares.

"Absolutely got to have flares," the sheriff said, towering high above the console, chewing his cigar. "Suppose you're in trouble, Kripstra, and you want some attention. You got to fire some flares."

"Flare gun?" Billy Boy asked.

No flare gun.

"This is for your own protection," Billy Boy said. "I know the fines are high but people got to learn to listen. Drop by anytime. Six violations at forty bucks each, let's see now."

"Two hundred and forty," Hairy Harry said.

"Thank you, Sheriff." Billy, taking his time, steady in spite of the boat's movements, filled in the ticket. He handed it over. "So you only got Europe dollars, I hear?"

Hairy Harry shifted into forward and pulled the gas handle a bit so that the powerboat could stay on course. "That's okay, Deputy, we can phone Boston for the rate of exchange."

"Plus forty percent," Billy Boy said, "for the trouble."

"Did you take the rowboat, Krip?" Hairy Harry asked.

Grijpstra mentioned Little Max and the ten dollars.

"Little Max has no right to rent out Big Max's dory."

"That'll be extra," Billy said. "Big Max will have to press charges. And he will. Isn't that right, Sheriff?"

"That's right," Hairy Harry said.

"Drop by anytime," Billy Boy said. "Anytime before tomorrow noon."

"That's when the bus leaves," Hairy Harry said. "We'll make sure you catch it. Bus back to Boston."

"After you've paid the fines and all," Billy Boy said.

The twin Johnson outboards roared and the powerboat turned, spraying Grijpstra with her wake.

Grijpstra rowed. The waves had grown with the strengthening breeze and it was hard to keep the dory from veering sideways. Every time it did, some water splashed against the hull and into the boat. Bar Island appeared and disappeared. There were shreds of fog. Grijpstra saw treetops through veils of froth, and purple rocks and ledges, gleaming as waves pulled back after crashing wildly. Large sea gulls with black wings and white bodies, effortlessly poised against the gale, cackled mockingly at his feeble effort to manipulate the slippery oars. A seal's head appeared, bald and round, with whiskers sprouting widely to each side. The eyes stared ghoulishly from deep sockets. The sea mammal's body, shimmering in sunlight that broke briefly through fog, raised itself vertically from a watery valley. The seal blew loudly. A greeting maybe or just clearing its nostrils? Grijpstra nodded. "How are you doing?" The seal, overwhelmed by this human response, tumbled over sideways and disappeared into his liquid world, like a clown who, after having been hilarious for a while, feels obliged to extinguish himself comically. Grijpstra, appreciating the show, rested on his oars. Low tide, at full force now, combined with strong winds to swoosh the dory along Bar Island and through the passage between Bar and Squid Islands. Grijpstra rowed on, exhausted now, with no effect.

A bizarre-looking building with sloped tiled roofs, two above, two below, the top one ending in a spire, peeked out of the pines. Grijpstra thought he couldn't have reached China yet. A wave raised the dory so that Grijpstra could see the ocean ahead, stretching, he remembered, not to China but back to Europe, to Nellie, to comforts, to survival, to ideas he would never realize now.

Although he felt impossibly tired and dizzy, he still made a show of working the oars. Why? To impress Nellie, facing him from the dory's back seat. Nellie looked pretty in a white dress and straw hat. Like the day they'd gone out on the Amstel River together.

The successful lover knows how to amuse his beloved.

"These waves are from the Far East, Nellie, as painted by—who was it? Hokusai? Hokusai waves, remember the reproduction I showed you? I wanted to use that wave in an Amsterdam canal, with dead ducks on top."

"HenkieLuvvie," Nellie said tenderly.

"Hokusai waves can swallow your house at Straight Tree Canal, Nellie."

Nellie laughed. Funny HenkieLuvvie!

So he was putting it on a bit maybe. "Well, they can swallow your bicycle shed."

A birch canoe passed, paddled by a smiling dog-faced woman. Then the forty-foot-long and forty-year-old cabin cruiser *Kathy Three* appeared, big and just sturdy enough to weather the weather. The vessel's eight-cylinder diesel thumped on relentlessly while the short skipper, Flash, his hairdo standing up in the wind, and equally short first mate, Bad George, his plastic face emotionless, looked the other way, sweeping the rough sea with binoculars, missing the dory bobbing out of sight between waves.

The dog, Kathy Two, small, blackish gray except for her blond face and feet, did see Grijpstra, and jumped about the bridge, waving long mustaches and eyebrows, barking shrilly. "Thar she blows," captain and mate shouted at each other.

The *Kathy Three* stopped and backed up a bit. A triple

hook, attached to a good length of thin rope, whizzed toward the dory's bow. Bad George, shouting through what Grijpstra took to be a papier-mâché mask and leaning across the railing, held out both hands. Grijpstra, wet through and through, holding his bag firmly like a bureaucrat out in the rain, was hoisted aboard. The dory itself followed. Kathy Two, jumping and sliding about the slippery deck, welcomed her wet guest. Passenger and dog were directed to the front cabin, where Grijpstra lay down on a cot and Kathy Two jumped up, putting a paw on his chest and her face on his arm, growling pleasantly.

"Damn dog usually don't like nobody," Bad George said, bringing hot coffee. The mug rattled against Grijpstra's teeth as he took in the cabin, resting place of broken and rusted tools, worn rope reinforced with tape, generic dog food and baked beans in large cans, dented fuel containers, and well-used engine parts. The cabin was clean, however, like the kitchen behind it, where scoured pots hung from hooks swaying between bunches of onions, a smoked ham, dried fish, and net bags filled with vegetables and potatoes.

Flash Farnsworth came to check his catch too. "You could have been swamped by them big waves, you know," Flash said. "Good thing Aki kept calling. Radio was acting up again, we didn't hear her for a while. How're you feeling?"

Grijpstra felt cold, hungry, his legs hurt, his head was throbbing. He didn't think this Hobbit was real. Flash did have hairy long toes, curling out of his sandals. He wore gray overalls with a yellow silk scarf, torn and dirty. He must have found the scarf, Grijpstra thought, lost by a tourist, blown into a tree. Flash didn't seem the kind who would buy silk scarves. His gray-and-white beard was shapeless, like a cloud blown against his face. The hair wafted up into his eyes. When he spoke, irregular teeth glinted.

There was shouting from the bridge, and stamping on the cabin's roof. Flash limped away. Grijpstra, moving painfully, tried to ignore Kathy Two. The little dog jumped about, thrusting up long thin ears, that, pink inside like festive pennants, stood out perpendicularly from her small furry face. She wagged a ragged tail.

"Invitation to the dance?" Grijpstra asked.

The dog yapped happily. Grijpstra picked her up.

"I don't dance, dear." Grijpstra staggered on and climbed a rickety ladder to reach the bridge where Flash was turning a small rusted wheel, staring intently ahead, one hand on the gas lever.

"Tricky here," Bad George said. "Shoals. Can't see them. Flash's supposed to know them."

The ship inched ahead slowly, turning sharply around the far end of Squid Island, almost touching trees at times, then veering off again to give the coast a wide berth. Here and there Grijpstra saw underwater amber-colored shapes, some rounded off, some jagged, waving seaweed.

"Ugly fellers," Bad George said, "they'll rip out yer bottom."

"Easy," Flash told the boat, tugging his beard, the other hand clasped tightly around the wheel. "Easy, darling."

Then all was calm. *Kathy Three* even picked up a little speed, sailing nicely between Squid Island's tentacles, until the engine roared briefly, while Flash shouted, "Hard astern" at himself, pulling the gear lever back, before shifting into neutral and switching the engine off. The *Kathy Three* floated quietly toward the island's dock, where de Gier waited and waved, caught the mooring rope with a delicate gesture, and twisted it expertly around a wooden cleat.

De Gier swung himself across the railing and hugged Grijpstra. He stepped back. "You're wet." He smiled. "Had a nice trip? I would have come looking for you but I only have the dinghy here." He patted Grijpstra's shoulder. "And Aki said the *Kathy Three* was picking you up." He bowed to Flash, Bad George, and the dog.

There wasn't any expression, except the usual, which was blank, on Bad George's face. Flash's face, being mostly hair, didn't convey much either, although there could be twinkles in his eyes, which bulged a bit and were bloodshot from peering into direct or sea-reflected sunlight. The dog, looking down from the bridge, frowned furiously.

"Thanks again," de Gier said.

Chapter 6

"Better?" de Gier asked when Grijpstra emerged from the shower. "Ready for lunch? Noodles? I made some noodles. You like mackerel? I have some scallops too that Lorraine got skindiving. Crabmeat? Your favorite cocktail sauce? For starters you do like seafood, don't you?"

"I could be goddamn seafood myself," Grijpstra said.

There were explanations of course, there always were. De Gier had been listening on the CB's open channel all morning except for two brief periods when he thought he heard Mr. Bear rummaging about the pagoda. Bears on the Maine coast don't care to show themselves much. Bear hunting is a sport, practiced diligently by experts such as Sheriff Hairy Harry and Deputy Billy Boy. De Gier wanted to photograph Mr. Bear with his new Nikon. He'd rigged up wires on the beach that Mr. Bear would touch if he showed up where he had climbed ashore before, at daybreak, a week ago, when de Gier happened to be awake, meditating on the cliffs, without the Nikon.

Something touched the wires twice that morning, triggering the alarm. Must have been foxes.

"Don't you carry your radio?" Grijpstra asked.

It wasn't a battery-operated CB. You had to plug it into the wall. "See?" De Gier demonstrated.

"First the goddamn deputy called in to tell you I was here," Grijpstra said, "and then the goddamn restaurant called in that I was here, and you were looking for a *bear?*"

Chance, happenstance . . . things go wrong sometimes, this is earth, a planet beyond human understanding, de Gier was truly sorry. "Okay?"

Not okay.

De Gier was sorry Grijpstra felt that way. So how was El Al? Wasn't Ishmael a card? Katrien had written that the commissaris's inflamed leg joints were a trifle better. True? Would Grijpstra care for lobster for dinner?

Grijpstra shoveled down fried noodles and pickles. He felt a bit better, he could maybe imagine that he didn't dislike de Gier. This was like long ago, when he avoided Mrs. Grijpstra by staying over at de Gier's suburban apartment, which faced parks front and back. De Gier was a good cook, using herbs he grew on his balcony, serving choice dishes with a welcoming flourish.

Grijpstra's tone of voice was almost pleading, "So how

come you said I could row the distance and when I tried I almost died?"

"From the Point," de Gier said, "it's only a quarter of a mile." He explained, "There's a peninsula south of Jameson and it bends this way." Hadn't Grijpstra seen the Point from Ishmael's plane? Ishmael lived at the Point. Didn't Ishmael show it to him from his airplane?

"I never got that," Grijpstra said. "There's the harbor just outside Beth's Diner, there are dories. Your island is visible from the harbor. . . ."

"No," de Gier explained. From Jameson Harbor to Squid Island was quite a few miles. Nobody in his right mind would ever try it. Only the stupid maybe.

"Stu-pid?" Grijpstra asked, lowering his fork, pointing his fork.

Well, kind of silly, de Gier said. And then somebody at the diner, probably Aki, was supposed to . . . lovely Aki, Akiapola'au . . . named after the vulture finch of her native islands of Hawaii . . .

"Vulture finch." Grijpstra glared. "No such thing."

"Please," de Gier said. "Change your coordinates. We aren't at home. Mr. Bear visits this island, and there's such a thing as a vulture finch in Hawaii." De Gier smiled. "You liked the lady? Aren't you pleased you came? Something else, eh?"

Grijpstra had carried his bowl of noodles to the window and was looking at the peninsula shore, which was, indeed, close. He was eating again.

"You liked Akiapola'au?"

"The vulture finch is lesbian," Grijpstra said.

De Gier stared.

"Isn't she?" Grijpstra asked. "So is Beth. I saw it. I always do."

"So?"

Grijpstra shrugged.

"Are you a sexist now?" de Gier asked.

"Please," Grijpstra said. "We've gone through this before. I was New Age before the Age was New. Sexism means that one sex thinks it's superior to the other. That's negative. I'm definitive."

"You're negative," de Gier said. "I asked whether you like Aki and you say, 'She's lesbian.'"

"Not that way." Grijpstra stopped slurping noodles. "I said, 'She's lesbian.'"

"With that kind smile?"

Grijpstra stopped slurping again. He swallowed. "With that kind smile."

"So you like Akiapola'au?"

"I like Akiapola'au fine."

"And Beth?"

Grijpstra nodded. "I like Beth fine too." He pointed his fork at de Gier. "It's you I don't happen to care for right now."

"I care for you," de Gier said. "I had made arrangements. If I wasn't at the restaurant when you arrived—and I probably wouldn't be since I didn't know how long Ishmael would take to get you here from Boston—then Beth was to call the *Kathy Three*. If she couldn't raise Flash and Bad George, either Beth herself or Aki was supposed to drive you to the Point, and you could row yourself from there. Beth told you so. She was busy, she asked you to wait a few minutes, but you wandered off, and then there you were rowing out into the bay, with a gale building up and low tide sucking like crazy. She sent the sheriff after you, but he came back, saying you didn't want to be picked up, which she found hard to believe, so she eventually managed to raise the *Kathy Three*."

"So you're telling me I was in good hands?" Grijpstra reported on his meeting with the sheriff's powerboat.

De Gier was nodding.

"What are you nodding for?"

"Another complication I didn't foresee," de Gier said. "There's drug traffic here. Maybe they think I'm interested. Now maybe they think you're interested too."

"Who's *they?*"

"Probably everybody," de Gier said. "There's marijuana growing on all the islands and there's more coming in by boat, and there's probably hard stuff too, being flown in all the time."

"And the sheriff is in on that?"

"Please," de Gier said.

"Please what?"

De Gier gestured. "Remember Amsterdam? Remember any possible drug being available at any possible time at any possible place and nearly four thousand policemen running around keeping the distribution going? You've heard of capitalism? Of supply and demand? If we don't do it someone else will? May as well be us? I mean, after all, who is in charge here?"

"Not all four thousand of them," Grijpstra said.

"Most all of them, some way or other."

"Not us."

"So the situation gets confusing," de Gier said. "If cops are supposedly against that sort of thing, but most of them are kind of all Hup Ho let's do it . . ."

"I almost got lost at sea because you told these killers here that you and I used to be cops?" Grijpstra asked. "That was brilliant. Were you trying to impress the ladies?"

"What should I tell the ladies?" de Gier asked. "That I was a needlecraft salesman? A former copper from Amsterdam chooses to live in the Twilight Zone. So what? What do Lorraine and Aki care? 'So where is Amsterdam? Amsterdam, Ohio?'"

"Where's Ohio?"

"Inland America," de Gier said. "They only know about their own country here. 'Europe? Europe where?'"

Grijpstra put down his bowl carefully, grabbed de Gier by the flaps of his neat bush jacket carefully, shook de Gier forcefully. "Why did you tell them you used to be a cop?"

There was an explanation, of course, wasn't there always. De Gier gently disengaged himself, served coffee, used his soothing voice, reminded Grijpstra that he, de Gier, had been to Jameson, Maine, before. To help out the commissaris to help out his sister, who, suddenly widowed, and being a helpless person, had to be repatriated forthwith. At the time de Gier had met some great people—the sheriff . . ."

"Hairy Harry?" Grijpstra asked. "You *knew* Hairy Harry?"

Another sheriff. Sheriffs come, sheriffs go. "Do you mind?" de Gier asked. "Can I go on? Can I explain this to you? You're a private detective now, you've taken on the job, you've got to protect yourself, you need all the information you can get. You're out in the open. Remember what the holy man said."

"All holy men are frauds," Grijpstra said.

"Why?"

Grijpstra shrugged. "Because there's nothing holy."

"This fraudulent holy man I refer to," de Gier said, "saw God, and he came back to tell us that things are the way they are because God is not a nice man. He said God is not our uncle."

"Flash Farnsworth is nice," Grijpstra said, "and Bad George is nice. And that dumb dog is nice too." He paused so de Gier could serve dessert. He spoke through a mouth filled with ice cream. He ate. "Who is not nice here? The sheriff. Who else?" He pointed his spoon at de Gier. "Who came here to murder girlfriends?"

"During my previous visit here," de Gier said "I met the hermit Jeremy. I thought he knew what I wanted to know. I didn't come here to murder girlfriends."

"Jeremy lives on this island?" Grijpstra asked.

De Gier smiled sadly. "As I said, God, not being my uncle, cannot be helpful. The search has to be chaotic. There are thousands of islands here. This is not Jeremy's island and Jeremy is long dead. Maybe he got it, maybe he lost it. What's for sure is that he was getting old and feeble and the town voted to place him in a home, so to escape he did what you almost did this morning . . ."

Grijpstra lowered his spoon. "Hermit Jeremy rowed away never to be seen again?"

"That's correct."

"Planned?" Grijpstra asked.

"Planned."

"What would it be like if you planned it?" Grijpstra asked. "I didn't plan and I saw lots of stuff."

"Hallucinating?"

"Nellie in a hat, waves by Hokusai swamping the bicycle shed, a dog-faced woman paddling a canoe."

"Farnsworth's mother." De Gier began to clear the table. "I live here for months preparing for the breakthrough and see nothing; you've hardly arrived, and you see it all."

"Not that you sent Ishmael to meet me," Grijpstra said. "Because I didn't see that and because Ishmael pretended the meeting was accidental so he could ask some questions. About you, for instance. He doesn't trust you."

"Ishmael knows nothing about Lorraine disappearing," de Gier said.

"Who is the detective here?" Grijpstra asked. "Fill me in on Ishmael. How long have you known him?"

"Ishmael met me last time I was here."

"What did he do then?"

"Drunk preacher?" de Gier asked. "That was the impression I got at the time. He said so himself too. Addicted to God and liquor. We met in Jeremy's cabin. Ishmael said he was giving it all up."

"Alcohol?"

"The securities," de Gier said. "As Ishmael saw them. Jeremy had to help him out." De Gier cheered up. "I tell you, Henk, that's where the way out has to be. Away with it all." De Gier looked pensive. "Including the guru, the guide, kick them over the precipice. But . . ."

"But . . . ?"

"The guide, the hermit has to show you where the precipice is."

Grijpstra looked stern. "So you can kick her off the cliffs? Lorraine was the guru?"

De Gier shook his head.

Grijpstra stared.

"Lorraine was a nice woman," de Gier said.

"Back to firmer ground," Grijpstra directed. "More about Ishmael. The man is too smart for his own good. Why his interest in what brings me here?"

"Ishmael?" de Gier asked. "Ishmael is okay."

"The plane was clean," Grijpstra said. "Since I quit BC smoking I can smell narcotics. Your sheriff also found nothing. Ishmael mentioned crossing borders. Bringing in aliens maybe?"

"You're accusing Ishmael of something?"

"You're being accused," Grijpstra said, "of murder. You're being blackmailed. Any connection with Ishmael perhaps?"

"You've got Flash and Bad George," de Gier said.

"They didn't ask me questions. They saved me."

"Ishmael," de Gier said, "flies his plane to see Mohawks in Canada and Mayas in Mexico, like Jeremy used to. Indians who practice shamanic wisdom."

"You visit Indians too?"

"I thought I no longer needed teachers."

"Organized shamanism," Grijpstra rubbed his thumb and index finger. "A profitable business these days."

"Ishmael doesn't care for money."

"Please," Grijpstra said. "Forget your nonsense for a moment. Do it for me, because we are friends. Pretend we're back in law enforcement. We study society's other side. We investigate those who profit by illegally taking from others. We concentrate on criminal untruth. Why didn't Ishmael tell me you sent him? Is he hiding a secret? What does he do for money?"

"Fixes marine diesel engines," de Gier said. "Does a good job, makes good money."

"Lots of kids?" Grijpstra asked. "A gambling habit? Uninsured ailments?"

"Healthy bachelor, lives alone," de Gier said.

"The past?" Grijpstra asked. "Molesting boys during Bible study?"

"He likes Aki."

"Who doesn't?" Grijpstra asked. "You two are pals? Ishmael visits here?"

"Yes. I visit him too. He plays piano."

"Expensive hobbies?"

"Collects valueless objects he displays in a four-story former cannery, an ancient building on the Point that he got for free somehow. I say . . ."

"You say?"

"You did understand," de Gier said, "that I sent him to Boston to collect you?"

"Right," Grijpstra said, looking around. "Nice place you have here."

De Gier agreed. The pagoda seemed to be the best choice for a well-funded seeker of truth, out of several vacation homes rented out by Bildah Farnsworth. This temple-like structure was the work of Goldy Yamamoto, a New York architect, designed along neo-Chinese lines. Yamamoto also believed in supplying all comforts: pumped spring water, air-conditioning and oil heat, fireplaces, automated kitchen. And Yamamoto had finished it off nicely. The inside wainscoting was orange-tinged pine, the beams were redwood, the floors western oak. Tall windows with wide windowsills offered views of seascapes and other islands. The apparently simple furniture was Quaker inspired, expensive, labor intensive. Coffee tables were made from varnished driftwood. The rugs were Oriental. A large abstract painting, obviously inspired by the local coast, calmed the mind with easy strokes of green on gray, pale blues for water, a white splash for a sail.

"Money buys good art," de Gier said. "The place was custom-built for an investment banker, a practicing Taoist, a man who, by losing his ego, became the flow of money himself."

"Bankrupt and out of a job now?" Grijpstra asked.

"Right."

"Nice," Grijpstra said. "How much are you paying?"

"Five hundred."

"A month?"

"A week."

"To who?"

"To Bildah," de Gier said. "Bildah Farnsworth picked it up when junk bonds crashed. He'll make a bundle when the present slump is over and property like this becomes marketable again."

"You know about Bildah building Hairy Harry a palace at half cost?"

De Gier laughed. "Ishmael told you. Sure. Harry had his drug profits laundered. Bildah is The Man here."

"Local business wizard?"

"Local everything," de Gier said. "Puppeteer in chief of the Twilight Zone. Checks on the game Hairy Harry and Billy Boy are playing, owns most of the ground Jameson is built on, holds the paper on the fishing fleet, cashes in on whatever is going."

Grijpstra shivered. "Bad guy, this Bildah?"

JANWILLEM VAN DE WETERING

"You cold?" de Gier asked. He got up to make coffee. Grijpstra followed him to the open kitchen. They watched the coffee machine perform. "Bad guy?" de Gier repeated. "I don't think so."

"Marital status?"

"Not married. Housekeeper for half days, bookkeeper a few days a week."

"Sex?"

"Housekeeper is old, bookkeeper has a relationship with Big Max."

"Describe Bildah."

"Peaceful?" de Gier asked. "Likes to hike beaches and trails. Bildah feeds the birds. Keeps a pet raven, name of Croakie, that flies around him." De Gier thought. "Haven't seen Croakie for a while."

"He who finances local activity with good collateral can enjoy his hiking," Grijpstra said. "Interest flows day and night. Subject do any work himself?"

"Rakes his paths," de Gier said. "Chops his firewood. Picks up shells on the beach. Talks to his raven. Croakie flies upside down on request."

Grijpstra sat down, nursing his coffee. He looked serious. "You know, you and I think we got this thing licked now but don't you believe we're still too busy? I keep thinking I am. I saw a little farm for sale the other day, close to the city. Derelict building, might fix it up a bit. Could rake the path maybe, keep a chicken or two, do nothing much else."

"You'd have nothing to keep you from facing the riddle."

"I'd get depressed?"

"Sure," de Gier said.

"Bildah doesn't mind facing the riddle?"

De Gier didn't think so. "The superior man?" de Gier suggested. "Could be, you know."

"Figured out the riddle?"

"Why not?" de Gier said.

"You really think anyone has?"

"Wouldn't surprise me," de Gier said. "There must be some around. Think of it. They would be sly, live alone, be well off, be quiet, smile a lot, enjoy simple pleasures. We can't all be stupid."

Grijpstra shook off the image. "Okay. Bildah Farnsworth, relative of Flash Farnsworth?"

"Distant relative. There are not too many families here, the local structure is kind of incestuous. They all have the same names. Beth is a Farnsworth too. There are a few Scottish names, McThis, McThat. Bad George is a Spade, lots of Spades around too."

"Living off the proceeds of evil," Grijpstra said. "Bildah, I mean. A superior man does not live off evil."

"Define evil."

Grijpstra put his mug down. "Pushing women down cliffs. What other evil did you get yourself into? I've been sending you five thousand dollars monthly. You've been spending all that?"

"I pay the rent," de Gier said. "I keep a car at the Point, a nice Ford, rented. I bought the dinghy I use for crossing the channel. That was two thousand. Groceries don't come cheap here, say a hundred a week. There's the sound equipment and the records I've been sending away for. Akiapola'au comes out to do the housework, she wants twenty an hour."

"We're talking dollars," Grijpstra said.

"Sure."

Grijpstra sighed. "I didn't bring any dollars. The Luxembourg bank didn't send your check this month because the manager there who knows my voice is on holiday. I was going to write them a letter to authorize the transfer but then you phoned. Got any cash?"

"A few hundred."

"Not enough." Grijpstra shook his head. "I'll have to get some."

De Gier laughed. "*We* are out of cash?" He prodded Grijpstra's chest. "But that's *crazy*."

"No dollars," Grijpstra said. "I brought lots of guilders. Hairy Harry went through my wallet. He seemed surprised." He rubbed his chin. "Ah. I almost forgot. The stewardess on the plane showed me a paper that said you can only bring in five thousand dollars in any currency and I brought eleven."

"The sheriff saw that?" de Gier asked.

"Yes."

"That's okay," de Gier said. "Hairy Harry only works for the county; federal regulations don't bother him much."

"It would be another reason to lean on us."

De Gier agreed.

Grijpstra kept rubbing his chin. "I'm supposed to leave by bus tomorrow." He reported on the Jameson Bay confrontation.

"You're right," de Gier said. "I should have kept a low profile here. I'll never learn. Drawing attention to myself, and to you too. And now there's Lorraine."

"Now there isn't Lorraine," Grijpstra said. "Does Ishmael know about that?"

De Gier didn't think so. "It's too early yet. Lorraine was a recluse herself, it'll be a while before she's missed. Want to do some site work?"

Grijpstra, wrapped in a towel, wearing a straw hat that belonged to de Gier and the slippers that Nellie had tucked in his bag, followed his host.

De Gier showed him the scene of the crime, a large granite cliff next to stone steps leading down to his dock.

De Gier was Lorraine, Grijpstra was de Gier. Grijpstra came, reeling and staggering, out of the pagoda's front door. De Gier stood, one foot on the highest step of the path, one foot on the cliff next to the path. De Gier, hungry for love, wanted to embrace Grijpstra. Grijpstra pushed de Gier away. De Gier fell over backwards.

De Gier held a black belt in judo. He rolled, jumped up lightly.

"But Lorraine hurt herself?" Grijpstra asked. He knelt near the spot where Lorraine, having been allegedly pushed, fell, and where, afterward, she had been allegedly kicked in the belly.

He did find a stain, not too clearly visible, a dried-up spot of a different, deeper red than the granite's natural pink-and-red shades.

"Has it rained since this happened?"

It hadn't.

Grijpstra leaned against the pagoda's balustrade. "Now then, show me what you did after Lorraine disappeared from your view."

De Gier stood on the veranda. "I was here." He pointed at the top stone step. "Lorraine stood there. I do recall shoving her. Next thing she wasn't there. I didn't hear her scream. Maybe she groaned. I recall some sound but I might have thought she was talking while walking down the steps."

"Not a lot of blood," Grijpstra said. "Maybe her clothes soaked it up." He coughed. "Vaginal? Possibly."

De Gier coughed too.

De Gier's cough irritated Grijpstra. "Irresponsible movie sheik on the rampage, even here." He glared. "You have a nasty habit there, my boy. And it isn't getting any better."

De Gier looked away. "Bad George claims she miscarried," he admitted. De Gier sat on the steps, jerking the ends of his mustache, baring his teeth that way. His voice seemed higher than normal. "I didn't ask him to produce proof either. Didn't want to know. That would have been in the boat, and they would have thrown it overboard, yes?"

"Baby could be yours?"

"I used condoms."

"Any breaks?"

"Yes," de Gier said.

"You've been here four months," Grijpstra said. "You were intimate straightaway? When did you meet Lorraine?"

"First day," de Gier said. "That answers both questions."

Grijpstra was shaking his head. "Lorraine was around forty? Did she mention pregnancy?"

"Irregularity," de Gier said. "She said it was normal, she'd been like that for a while. It seemed to bother her, though."

"So it's Flash and Bad George, who're trying extortion, who assert subject was pregnant."

"Who's *subject*?" de Gier asked. "This is Lorraine."

"Subject." Grijpstra slapped de Gier's shoulder. "Nothing is personal to me here. You're nothing but my client. If I cared I would be useless." He poked de Gier's chest. "We continue. The extortionists brought the body back. Let's see how they did that."

De Gier became Bad George, coming up the steep path from the little harbor below, carrying Lorraine's body lightly across his arms.

"Hmmm," Grijpstra said. "Not a heavy woman, I see."

"Slender," de Gier said. "Lovely body. Bit of a monkey face, though, wrinkled up, because of a bad marriage, divorce. She lived with her parents for a while, in a trailer park in Arizona. Parents own Bar Island over there, bought it as an investment when they were young, thought it would appreciate in value, which it didn't."

"Subject had money?"

"She was a biologist. Her university provided income. Subject had a grant to study birds here, and planned to teach in Boston later on. Bar Island is a sanctuary for terns, but there are fewer each year. She had to find out why."

"Why?"

"Sea gulls," de Gier said. "They're bigger than the terns and they keep taking the eggs or the young. Lorraine had statistics. She knew where the gulls breed and was proposing that she and Aki take their eggs."

"Aki is a biologist too?"

"Not as well-qualified as Lorraine."

"Sanctuary," Grijpstra said. "Subject thought she'd get a break from her divorce mess here." He looked at the island to the east, Bar Island. "Nice. So she wasn't really from around here?"

"New York, originally. This was the family's summer place, they used to camp out here, built a nice cabin. Her parents thought they might winterize the place and retire here but the mother got emphysema and Arizona has dry air."

"Smoker?"

"So subject said. The mother sucks cigarettes and oxygen at the same time from a cylinder she carries around. A cripple."

Grijpstra coughed painfully.

"How's your affliction?" de Gier asked.

"Doctor says I stopped just in time," Grijpstra said. "So subject really was a nature woman?"

"Sure." De Gier gestured. "Paddled a kayak to stay happy. Lived on health food. Lots of energy. The terns got boring and she started a paper on loons. She and Aki were out most mornings. Loons like daybreak."

"Loons?"

"Birds, water birds, fairly big," de Gier said. "You'll love them. Impressive patterns of black and white, with piercing red eyes. Endangered species but still abundant on Maine bays and lakes. Make unbelievable sounds, like opera singers who have gone beautifully crazy."

"Male opera singers?"

"Female opera singers."

"So what we have here is a lonely and sensitive fairly attractive female subject," Grijpstra said. "I'm familiar with your case history and profile." He clasped his hands in back of him and studied de Gier sternly. "Your modus operandi is that you make yourself available but you don't actively seduce. So subject came on to you. You told her okay, but nothing serious please; the human race is a mistake, you don't want to add to its numbers. You're in principle against homo sapiens but as you find yourself in human shape you'll go along with that for as long as the condition doesn't get too uncomfortable. You don't believe in relationships either but short-time lust can be exciting. If, on those conditions, subject is interested. . . . And so on. Yes?"

De Gier sighed affirmatively.

Grijpstra looked fatherly. "Rinus?"

"Henk?"

"Your attitude, does it ever make you feel guilty?"

De Gier looked away.

"You look guilty now."

"Lorraine is a nice woman," de Gier said.

"You don't believe subject is dead?"

De Gier got up, walked a few steps down, came up again. "Sure, she's dead. I saw her corpse."

"Now," Grijpstra said, "I'm only trying to ascertain whether you were out of your mind and in that state murdered Lorraine. Tell me, is this whole thing of yours here"— Grijpstra pointed at the pagoda, at heads of seals popping up out of the sea, at pine trees on cliffs, at de Gier himself—"a continuation of what you tried to do in New Guinea?"

De Gier nodded. "The shaman reminded me of Jeremy here."

"Shaman," Grijpstra said. "Sorcerer. Witch doctor. Did the medicine man suggest you should do drug-induced vigils?"

"He did," de Gier said. "There was an island there he would go to. He told me he would use music, dance, sing, take his preferred drugs, seek out animals, birds. Collect rocks, shells, driftwood. Make shapes."

"Exactly," Grijpstra said, "and your preferred drugs are bourbon and marijuana, which are easily available here, and this is an island, and your favorite music is Miles Davis's funk-jazz now and you have your own mini-trumpet, and everywhere in the pagoda I see your compositions of rocks and shells laid out, and you're trying to meet Mr. Bear, and the loons are singing."

"You can't quite call it *singing*," de Gier said.

"Something unique," Grijpstra said. "You mixed that in with all your other ingredients, and you finally work up to the final pitch. . . ."

"Maybe alcohol is not such a good idea," de Gier said. "The New Guinea shamans don't care for it but as I'd been using alcohol more or less successfully before I thought I might try. . . ."

Grijpstra was reverting to his police mode, being pleasant but firm. "After Lorraine fell, did you go after her and do some kicking?"

"So Farnsworth says."

"But he wasn't there."

"He and Bad George watched her die on the *Kathy Three*."

"And she said you had kicked her? Again and again? In her belly, so that she lost her baby?"

"Not in so many words."

Grijpstra nodded, as if all this were only too clear. "How about this theory to explain your motivation: Lorraine's interference with your experiment, with all that effort, first in New Guinea on the other side of the world and now here, to reach the fourth, the spiritual dimension, enraged you. The bourgeoisie, unwilling to see you escape, tries to pull you back to your original level. You fight back." Grijpstra patted de Gier's shoulder. "What do you think?"

De Gier mumbled.

Grijpstra kept a hand behind an ear.

"Could be, Henk."

"Now," Grijpstra said. "What about *this* theory? Would you admit to being bourgeois yourself, an ordinary, limited, petty true Dutchman? No? Bear with me a little longer. I say you're ordinary enough but you don't like that. You try to free yourself, be on your own, the lone cowboy. You can't do it, though. You submit to subterfuge, you replace your ordinary parents by a little less ordinary, but still quite ordinary folks, Katrien and the commissaris. You appoint me to replace your moralizing born-again Catholic sister as the older sibling. Meanwhile you stay what you always were, a self-seeking little boy reluctantly growing up as an emotionally retarded adult. Think of all those faxes from New Guinea—letters from summer camp, right? Trying to impress your parents and outdo your older sibling, me. It's all so obvious, Rinus. Remember that snapshot of you and the exotic girl on your moped?"

De Gier stood over Grijpstra, swinging his fists

through the air. "Outrageous, Henk . . . what the hell . . . where do you get that bull? That was a Kawasaki 2000, and the lady was Lieutenant Jennifer Jones of the Tobriands . . . a colleague at the time. . . ."

"But," Grijpstra said triumphantly, "but what happens here? You can't fool the subconscious, my boy. You always knew you were being silly. You dislike that. Now, by happenstance, you manage to impregnate Lorraine, and you're about to double your bourgeois aspect. You can't handle one of you and now there'll be two. Self-hatred can lead to suicide, but suicide, in your case, would be too heroic to expect. You can't kill yourself so you help Lorraine to have an accident so that she may lose your clone."

De Gier squeezed his face with both hands. His distorted features stared at Grijpstra.

"Yes?" Grijpstra asked.

"Dr. Shrinkski," de Gier said. "Go fuck yourself, Dr. Shrinkski."

Chapter 7

Ishmael, who showed up later in the afternoon, making his dinghy go backward by pushing the oars with short frantic movements, said it was a piece of cake. Always confront the enemy. Live free or die. Buy American. Reduce the deficit. The attitude doesn't always work but isn't bad in simple cases. He used de Gier's CB in the pagoda's living room. "This is Ishmael, Sheriff. Are you listening? Over."

The answer came through clearly. "Deputy Billy here. How may I help?"

"A question," Ishmael said. "You know I know a bit of the law, but I don't know all of the law."

"You don't know all of the law," Billy echoed.

Ishmael, turning the microphone off, looked at Grijpstra. "There's this book, *How to Take Care of Your Own*

Divorce in Maine, but it's hard to read. I can read the book, so I help folks out some. I've been doing that. Billy knows."

"Ishmael?" the radio asked.

"Also did a spell in the military police, Billy Boy knows that too."

Ishmael clicked on his microphone. "I was telling Krip here about the Constitution, Billy Boy. We the people. Maybe we better switch out of the open channel. This may take some time. Meet me on channel eighty?"

Ishmael turned the radio's dial and switched on the mike.

"Billy Boy?"

"Right here."

"Tell me, Deputy, if people have a complaint about you folks where should they take it? State police? The attorney general in Augusta? I'm a bit rusty on that."

"You got a complaint about the sheriff's office?"

"On behalf of an esteemed and well-connected tourist from a friendly white Protestant country," Ishmael said. "Remember Kripstra?"

"Just a minute now," Billy Boy said. "You hold on."

Hairy Harry's benign voice, avuncular, sounding concerned about others' welfare, made Grijpstra jump. "Sheriff here. What's this complaint, Ishy?"

"Criminal negligence," Ishmael said. "Is that the right term?" Ishmael released the microphone's button and smiled at Grijpstra.

"Sounds good to me, Ishy. You have a for-instance?"

"It's like the example you had last winter, Harry. The raped college girl who got left at the roadside, with five inches of snow and the temperature in the low teens and this Portland couple came by in the rental and they didn't stop and the girl froze to death. But they did phone you much later, from a motel somewhere. Remember charging that couple with criminal negligence? Recall the court case?"

"It's summer now," the sheriff said.

"Yep." Ishmael winked at Grijpstra. "Summer. You're right, Harry. But kind of chilly, especially on the water. And we had quite a wind, more of it offshore, and we had low tide rushing out like Boston traffic and we had our confused friendly tourist in a bare dory, trying to get to Squid Island, but being swept out to nowhere, and then we had you and Billy Boy, Jameson's finest, in the exercise of your duty to serve and protect, in a powerboat designed and equipped to do just that, financed by us taxpayers." Ishmael paused. "And *then* what happened?"

"How's Kripstra doing?" the sheriff asked.

"Badly shaken, Harry."

"Witnesses who would support this complaint?" the sheriff asked.

"Recall, Sheriff, that when you returned to shore you went to Beth's Diner, and talked to Beth herself, and to Aki too, and you said Kripstra didn't want any assistance. They didn't believe you, as any reasonable witness subpoenaed by the prosecution wouldn't. So what do we have now? Aki in court. Stating under oath that she radioed the skipper of the *Kathy Three* to save said tourist. And now we have old salts Flash and Bad George in court too, describing said tourist's condition. And now the district attorney questions victim Kripstra here, a former law enforcement officer, a skilled and reliable detective-adjutant out of the right side of Europe."

Ishmael watched the momentarily quiet CB.

"Hairy Harry? Over?"

"Yes, Ishmael," the sheriff said softly.

"So where do we go? The attorney general? You have a number I can call, Hairy Harry?"

"That won't be necessary," the sheriff said. "Tell the complainant from the right side of Europe that we're truly sorry. Me and Billy Boy thought that a citizen of a watery country like Holland might be used to . . . well . . . never mind now. Ishy, we were wrong. Tell Kripstra he doesn't have to come in tomorrow. Tell him he's our guest. Tell him to make sure that nothing happens to him that Billy and I don't want to happen to confused tourists. That'll be it for today."

"Good," de Gier said when Ishmael put the micro-phone down.

"Thank you," Grijpstra said.

Ishmael rowed back to the Point, taking Grijpstra along. The Tao-guided Wall Street investment banker had had no time to sink a telephone cable between shore and Squid Island and Grijpstra remembered he had made a promise.

Chapter 8

"Are you ready?" Katrien asked, her finger on the tape recorder that Nellie had brought in a few minutes earlier.

The commissaris, in a silk robe, exuding a pleasant fragrance of after-shave, sat in his study. A large map of the northern section of the Maine coast was stick-pinned to a board on his desk. His right hand, holding a sharpened pencil, hovered over the first page of a new notebook.

"I heard the tape," Katrien said. "Nellie played it for me. She asked all your questions. Don't you think Grijpstra will be annoyed if he finds out we're doing this?"

"No," the commissaris said. "I thought I would try and use Nellie-type questions but that would be complicated. I had to use my own. He answered them so he doesn't mind."

Katrien pressed the recorder's button.

"Nellie?" Grijpstra asked.

"Oh, HenkieLuvvie, I'm so pleased you called. Are you all right?"

"Just dandy, dear, just dandy."

"Did you get to de Gier?"

"Yes."

"Do you miss me?"

Katrien interrupted the tape. "She had to ask that too."

"That's fine," the commissaris said, waving at the interruption as if it were a mosquito. "That's fine, dear."

Katrien pushed the recorder on again. "So how is Rinus?" Nellie asked.

"Not so good."

"Is he crazy?"

"Not now."

"You think he was crazy?"

"He's been doing this New Guinea Papuan bone-through-the-nose stuff," Grijpstra said. "But that sorcerer who taught him, that shaman he's always talking about, that fellow probably knows what he's doing by himself on his island, and de Gier's level is more like a group thing out there in the bush . . ."

". . . under the banyan tree?" Nellie asked. "That's what Rinus said in his letters from New Guinea. Doesn't that sound romantic? I saw a banyan tree in the zoo, in the greenhouse. It's beautiful, with all those air roots . . ."

". . . it's regular Christmas trees here . . ."

". . . but Christmas trees are magic too, Henkie-

Luvvie, we have them right here in Holland, you don't have to go all that way to . . ."

"Listen," Grijpstra said, "this is a pay phone, you have to call me back. Write this down—01 207 . . ."

The recorder kept clicking, then came on again.

"HenkieLuvvie? Isn't this horribly expensive? Are you billing de Gier?"

"Don't worry about money."

"I do worry. HenkieLuvvie?"

"Yes?"

"Was de Gier crazy?"

"He could have been when he attacked subject. He has said as much."

"Does he remember kicking poor Lorraine?"

Katrien switched off. "Isn't Nellie clever?"

The commissaris waved impatiently. "The corpse, Nellie, the corpse . . ."

"HenkieLuvvie? Is de Gier sure he saw Lorraine's corpse?"

"Yes," Grijpstra said. "Everybody here is of some origin or other, from someplace else I mean, and Lorraine was Swedish, and she had that hair, very fair, almost white. Angel hair?"

"You like that, Henk? I could bleach mine a bit more."

"No Nellie, please. And she had those feet."

"Swedish feet?"

"Special feet. Very slender."

"The judges liked my feet. But my breasts . . ."

"Regular breasts," Grijpstra said. "And the breasts were not exposed. Bad George was carrying the body rolled up in a blood-soaked blanket."

"You're sure it was blood?" Nellie asked.

"Could have been water," Grijpstra said. "It was dark, de Gier was out of his mind. They told him it was blood and he freaked out as usual. Mr. 'Murder Brigade Detective.' Tsksh. Jesus." Grijpstra snarled. "So we have recognizable hair hanging out one side of the blood-soaked blanket and recognizable bare feet hanging out the other and the body was dead."

"Wasn't de Gier too drunk to be sure?"

"No," Grijpstra said. "I do believe that angel-haired slender-footed body was dead. De Gier is too insistent. And don't forget he has seen hundreds of corpses in his time. There's something about dead bodies that makes them change into objects. Leftovers. Castoffs. De Gier may have been crazy but he knows about being dead."

Katrien switched off the recorder. "That's bad, Jan. No? I think that sounds bad."

"I'd like to hear the bad part again," the commissaris said. He was listening carefully when Katrien replayed the tape, leaning toward the recorder.

". . . but he knows about being dead," Grijpstra's hoarse voice said.

"Again, Jan?" Katrien asked.

"No, just carry on, dear."

"So what are you going to do, HenkieLuvvie?" Nellie asked.

"Find that corpse," Grijpstra said. "Flash and Bad George are trying some extortion. Rinus has been spending a lot of money so they think he's loaded. They gave him a big bill for saving me too, left it on the doorstep of the pagoda. You should see this place, Nellie. American wealth . . ."

"Saved you from what?" Nellie asked shrilly.

"Oh, I started rowing to Squid Island from the wrong place and there was a bit of a wind so they came looking for me and the dog spotted me—nice dog, Nellie, we should keep a dog too."

"Puppies poop and rip up carpets," Nellie said. "What makes you think that corpse is still there? Wouldn't they have burned it? Or dumped it overboard?"

"Extortionists do not destroy the evidence implicating their victim."

"So you find Lorraine's body," Nellie said. "Then what will you do?"

"I don't know, Nellie."

"You can't help a killer to escape."

"Something else," Grijpstra said. "There's a lot of drug traffic here. Imported and locally grown."

"Not your business, huh, HenkieLuvvie?"

"The sheriff's business," Grijpstra said.

"I should say so," Nellie said.

"That's not quite what I meant. . . . Oh, by the way,

Nellie, if you see the commissaris tell him that this hermit he and de Gier knew here, Jeremy, got old and sick and rowed himself into nowhere, but there's a disciple, a man called Ishmael."

"I don't like hermits, Henk. Hermits don't have enough to lose."

The commissaris winked at Katrien. She made a movement to stop the tape. He shook his head.

"Ishmael seems to be helpful," Grijpstra said. "And there's a woman who works in the restaurant here, a friend of Rinus's, who'll drive me to Boston to change my money. She's from Hawaii and she wants to go to Boston to see an exhibition of Hawaiian historical paintings. . . ."

"Henk!"

"I can't drive myself," Grijpstra said, "I get too sleepy, you know that."

"How old is this Aki, Henk?"

"Thirty-ish?"

"No! From Hawaii! They all swing their hips, and they're immoral. Remember that movie? How they crawled all over the sailors? And made them stay with them and that poor captain had to go home alone?"

"Aki's gay, Nellie. She lives with Beth, Beth owns the restaurant. It's all right, Nellie."

Katrien switched off the recorder. "After that, they're fighting. Poor Nellie. She's very upset about that gorgeous Hawaiian lady, Jan." She caressed his bald head, a little heavy-handedly. "Too bad you couldn't go."

Chapter 9

De Gier had gone ashore later in his own dinghy, a hand-crafted nutshell made out of thin cedar strips that sat high on the water. He joined Beth and Aki, plus Ishmael and Grijpstra, at the restaurant, where he arranged the journey to Boston. "Aki's car is a rustbucket, the doors are full of rainwater. They slosh when you bang them shut. You'd better take my car."

The rental, a shiny new four-door "Ford product," as Beth and Aki called it, impressed Grijpstra. Grijpstra remembered, from World War Two days in Holland, the time when there were no cars except German army vehicles. He also recalled the first American cars coming in after liberation: large shiny chariots that zoomed quietly on Holland's deserted highways, superior inventions from an advanced planet, benevolent robots symbolizing a luxurious beauty that had been beyond a child's imagination.

"Wow!" Grijpstra said when he first saw de Gier's rental. "Nice wheels."

"All yours," de Gier said.

"You guys must be rich," Aki said as she drove the car, cruise-controlled at sixty-five miles an hour, on Interstate 95, a highway that appeared like an endless park to Grijpstra. "Rinus just keeps that car sitting at the Point? At what? At forty bucks a *day?*"

"He had an inheritance," Grijpstra said, sitting back, fingers intertwined on his stomach, undergoing the pleasant repetition of a million trees, similar but never identical, with rock arrangements sloping down to the multilaned highway. He remembered a letter from De Gier that referred to the rocks along Interstate 95. De Gier, combining his interests in gardening and the surreal, wrote that the rocks might have been placed by Chinese monks. Grijpstra visualized that image: a thousand monks, in straw sandals, robes tucked into belts, practicing the art of shifting overweight rocks along a thousand miles of foreign roadway, in the hope of pleasing the deity within by abusing their emaciated bodies. But this was America, pleasing a different facet of that very same deity, and there were machines alongside the interstate, mechanical dinosaurs with long necks, daintily moving rocks about with their muzzles.

"See that?" Aki asked. "That dragline we just passed? Made in *Japan?*"

"Rains," Aki said a little later, looking sexy in a short leather skirt and a T-shirt printed with a design of bare-breasted Hawaiian dancers under palm trees. "Frost must have dislodged the granite. They're always working on this road. Rinus had an inheritance? Are you kidding? Isn't he lucky? So he can do all that traveling and gadding about."

"Yes," Grijpstra said.

"Watching nature out of his dinghy," Aki said. "You know what he paid for that dinghy? Over two thousand, and that's secondhand. It took two men a month to build it." She shook her head. "He says I can have it when he leaves."

"Lucky with investments too," Grijpstra said. "Rinus just keeps making money. A golden thumb."

"You're kidding."

I'm kidding, Grijpstra thought.

There were more miles sliding by. Grijpstra liked the well-behaved traffic controlled by an occasional gleaming cop car. He told Aki this was the way it should be, just a few people in a million square miles, just a few rules, the mini-mum of good-looking law enforcement, nice food in road restaurants, attractive wildlife grazing along the highways' shoulders and well beyond in bordering fields. He pointed at long-tailed magpies fluttering between white pines, at a large dark shape cantering lightly across a glade. "What the hell was that?"

"Moose," Aki said. "There are lots of moose in Maine, more now that we've killed off the wolf. Moose are bigger than camels, you know. Moose are next on the list. You can get a license to shoot them now. One of the state's new attractions. Five hundred bucks a pop. They're easy: they'll wait for you, you can walk up to them, say hello, blast them between the eyes."

"Will there be any left?"

"Maybe," Aki said. "Hairy Harry and Billy Boy will stuff the last one for target practice." She touched Grijpstra's knee. "Or it'll be like the nature movies. See these moose?" She deepened her voice. "Behold the broad flattened antlers. North America's largest deer. This is rare footage, folks, taken of the last-known herd some ten years ago." Aki snarled. "And then you hear shots and you see the final moose crumple and fall, breathe blood."

"No," Grijpstra said. He raised his hands in defense. "Please, Aki."

"I'm sorry." She pulled her hand back to the wheel. "It's my name, it makes me ghoulish. You know my full name?"

Grijpstra closed his eyes, frowning as he searched his memory. "Akiapola'au?"

She laughed. "That's awesome, Krip. They can't even remember it in Hawaii. You know what it means?"

"Vulture finch?"

"Who told you that?" She shook her head in disbelief. "You have a special interest in me?"

"You told me," Grijpstra said. "First time we met. I'm a detective. I'm trained to recall data."

"I'm data to you?"

Grijpstra shrugged. "Just a habit. Tell me about the Hawaiian vulture finch."

"It's a lie," Aki said. "I tell it to make myself interesting. Nobody knows about Hawaiian birds here but there is such a thing at home as a vulture finch."

"There are no regular vultures in Hawaii?"

"No big land birds at all," Aki said. "Hawaii is nowhere. Nowhere is too far for big birds to fly to, but little birds were blown over by hurricanes. There's this little cute-looking bird that you'd swear is a finch that feeds on dead bodies. That's how I found out life isn't Walt Disney. I was out as a kid playing and there was a dead man in a field, a drunk who got hurt and who dragged himself out there, and the body was crawling with gorgeous little birds, gorging themselves."

"Yecch . . ."

"But why? It's not really revolting." Aki asked. "There's no biological reason for vultures to be big."

"You know about biology?" Grijpstra asked as the car slowed down. There was a commotion further along the interstate.

"My major subject," Aki said, "at the University of Honolulu, and now I serve eggs over easy to the wild men of Jameson, Maine. It's not a pretty story, Krip."

Traffic had stopped. A car had left the road ahead, at a high speed probably, for it had rolled over a few times. And it had been a while ago because an ambulance was now backing up to the wreck, policemen were directing traffic, and a helicopter hovered above.

Eventually traffic moved again. "Makes me think of Beth's father," Aki said. "It was last winter. Big Daddy'd been to the grave of Beth's sister. The man was eighty years old and almost blind but every few days he made himself take flowers to the cemetery, to alleviate some guilt. Apparently he had maltreated the girl. Then Big Daddy disappeared. Nobody could figure it out. He'd bought the flowers at Gary's Greenhouse behind Main Street, and Gary had seen him drive off toward the cemetery, which is along a straight road through the forest west of town. The flowers were found on the grave but Big Daddy never came back."

"Maybe a good way to go," Grijpstra said.

"You figured it out?" Aki asked.

Grijpstra sat quietly while the Ford product sped along. "Getting hungry, Krip?"

He was but he didn't want to eat at any of the fast food places that they passed once in a while: slabs of concrete behind plastic signs. Beth had known of an inn with gourmet food and Grijpstra read the map that she had marked with arrows, giving Aki clear directions.

"Aren't we a deadly combination?" Aki said when they sat on the inn's terrace, facing a pond with a collection of exotic ducks and geese.

"And how do you like these gorgeous fowl, Krip?"

Grijpstra knew the birds' names.

"You took biology too, Krip?"

JANWILLEM VAN DE WETERING

He told her he painted birds, in the Dutch Golden Age tradition, a time when Dutch merchants liked to keep exotic fowl on their country estates and had them portrayed for extra glory.

"And now you see them in America. More Belgian steamed mussels? More French bread? This is America, Krip, we indulge every desire. You don't have to go anywhere to get anything, it's all right here. You solved the puzzle yet, Krip?"

Grijpstra thought so. Beth's father, when he disappeared, was eighty years old and nearly blind so he wouldn't have been able to drive on unfamiliar roads. He had driven home after leaving the cemetery, where else would he have gone? But he hadn't gotten home. On the way home he had become sick or had fallen asleep, like the driver of the overturned car on the interstate just now. A stroke or a cardiac arrest made him slump over the wheel and stamp on the gas at the same time. Being an old man he was driving an old car, a tank of the gas-guzzling type. The car had left the road and barreled into the forest, which, like most in northern Maine, grew up to both sides of the rural road. The car flattened saplings and brushes until stopped by a tree trunk. There the car sat. The saplings behind it bent back.

"What about that big old Packard's massive tracks?" Aki asked.

"This happened in winter?"

"Yes."

"So there might have been snow," Grijpstra said. "Snow covered the car's tracks after the car entered the forest."

"You're good," Aki said.

Grijpstra looked pleased. "That's what happened?"

"Exactly."

"The sheriff sent out search parties?" Grijpstra asked.

"He saw ravens circling the next morning," Aki said, "and an eagle. Eagles are scavengers too. And the big sea gulls. They have cruel eyes. They go for your eyes first, they don't wait for you to die."

"Was Beth's father dead before the birds found him?" Grijpstra asked.

"Oh yes," Aki said, "there was an autopsy. The heart attack must have killed Big Daddy straight off."

Grijpstra enjoyed the cream pie Aki ordered, a Florida pie made from limes, foreign to Maine. He dozed in the car until, close to Boston, the traffic became noisy.

"Motel out of town?" Aki asked. "Hotel in town? Hotels will be expensive. Any preference, Krip?"

He waved his credit card. "Nothing but the best."

Aki had heard about the Parker House being good. "But *very* expensive. You really don't mind?"

He didn't. He liked the skyscrapers lining the parkway and the way Aki handled the car, driving close to cabs so that she could ask their drivers for directions.

"Hold it Krip." The car shot across a sidewalk and dived into a garage. "This is it. Out you go."

Bellboys took over, parking the car, carrying luggage, driving the elevator, ushering them through the lobby.

Grijpstra ordered separate suites. Aki canceled that. "One suite will do." He protested. "I'll get lonely, Krip. The big city reminds me."

He worried. There was Nellie, there was disease, but then there was safe sex, but he didn't want safe sex either. Besides, why *not* separate suites? What could a thirtyish extraordinarily attractive homosexual Polynesian female want with a sixty-year-old slightly obese white heterosexual male? Information? Information about what?

He missed de Gier. De Gier, while roaming the alleys of good old Amsterdam, would have had something smart to say about the situation. Now de Gier, auto-induced schizophrenic meddler with fourth-dimensional reality, was a goddamn suspect himself.

Aki and Grijpstra talked over dinner, at an age-old oyster bar in Boston's harbor district, eating quahogs stuffed in their shells, root beer for Grijpstra, tonic and lime for Akiapola'au, served by old, ugly, rough but not uncaring waitresses.

"No alcohol, Krip?"

"I can't smoke anymore," Grijpstra said, tapping his chest.

"Can't drink without smoking?"

"True," Grijpstra said. "Yourself?"

"I'm alcoholic.

He left it at that, watching Boston women. He thought Bostonian women looked like women from The Hague— quiet, dressed with a kind of in-between taste that wouldn't commit them one way or another.

"Want to know when I stopped?" Aki asked.

"Being alcoholic?"

She laughed. "I will always be *that*. Stopped drinking, I mean."

"Tell me."

"When I came to Maine two years ago," Aki said. "You want to know why?"

"Tell me."

"You sure?"

Grijpstra was sure.

"Because of hopping backwards up to a urinal in an army barracks restroom with my clothes off and shy soldiers staring."

"I see."

"Do you?" She laughed. "Of course. You're a detective. I had to pee so bad and I had no idea where I was and I was so pleased I found that toilet and then it was too high and the soldiers came in and they didn't get it either." She laughed again. "It's the sort of tale you hear at AA meetings. They keep being told in the hope that they'll go away in the telling but they don't, and then you want to drink again."

"Or not," Grijpstra said, smiling.

"Never," Aki said, "never, Krip." She reached across

the table and patted his hand. "You're such a nice man. Isn't this fun? You and I together away from everything. Are you taking me anywhere good afterward?"

"Music?" Grijpstra asked.

"There's good music in Boston, Krip."

"We'll do that," Grijpstra said. "Now tell me about how you got to that army barracks."

"Begin at the beginning? You'll still take me out even if I depress you?"

"I'll still take you out."

The beginning was at a Kona Coast coffee plantation on the big island of Hawaii, idyllic still: barefoot brown children playing in the surf and singing—"I can hold high notes, Krip"—and the volcano lighting up the beach at night and Aki's parents the nicest ever and good marks at school. There was the cat, Poopy, and the dog, Snoopy, and papayas and avocados on the garden trees and dancing in the shopping mall with Aunt Emma beating her gourds and shuffling her big soft feet, coaching all the little kids of the neighborhood, any kind of little kids, some of them so white you could hardly see them in the light, some black as midnight, all the native kids golden all over.

Grijpstra laughed.

"You like that, Krip?" She sighed. She wasn't going to tell him the rest of it, then she did. Her father started up with an older ugly woman, nobody knew why, *he* didn't know why, and he lost his job. And they were in a trailer that had been on fire and was still blistered outside. Her father was drinking and beating up people, his car got dented, he wasn't even proud that Aki got a full scholarship in Honolulu and then she started drinking too. Dope, too, everything. Honolulu is the Far East and marijuana is a cash crop in Hawaii.

"Heroin?"

Not too much, she didn't like the needle but it liked her, like the boyfriend did. He with the different faces, who took her to the mainland to keep him in a style he wasn't accustomed to at all, by taking weird men in and out of motel rooms, for years, all the way across the continent, to Maine in the end, where the boyfriend (she kept getting away from him and he kept coming back in different guises, colors, ages) assumed a military face and she was in the barracks with her clothes off, jumping up, trying to reach that china bowl screwed against the wall out of reach, with all the jocks watching. They weren't even laughing, they were too embarrassed.

"Alcohol?"

"What else?" Aki asked. "It got me arrested then, but I was out of it. The cops might have released me into my family's custody but there wasn't any family left so I finished up with some nuns."

"That's when you became lesbian?"

"I always preferred my own side. With Hawaiians the gay have their own place." Her hand was on his again. "You mind?"

Grijpstra said he was from Amsterdam, which was like . . .

"Key West?"

He didn't know where that was.

"Provincetown?"

Never heard of Provincetown.

"San Francisco?"

Grijpstra remembered watching TV pictures of mostly beautiful men and women waving protest banners down steep streets and thinking at that moment that the New World was behind the times. In Amsterdam it was getting to be the other way around, with a heterosexual majority trying to move out from the shade of guilty regularity. "Yes," he said happily, "San Francisco."

They were both smiling, having a wonderful time. "Akiapola'au," Grijpstra asked, "are you and Beth watching the coast for drug trafficking?"

"Daddy-O," she said, her face hardly cooling, "you don't have to be so clever." She leaned over to peck his cheek. "I was about to tell you all about it."

Chapter 10

"So what else is new?" de Gier asked Grijpstra across a table at Beth's Diner, where he was positioning the table's honey bear within a circle of sauce bottles. "I could have told you that. Isn't that the way law enforcement works? After Aki was treated at the Hospital of the Loving Little Lamb in Lordsville, the cops must have jumped her, with a shitload of charges to back them up. She had been running around all over the country, being bad . . ."

"Did she tell you how bad?"

De Gier waved vaguely. "Overdrawn checks, theft of rental cars, stealing from johns, drug charges, and"—he dropped his eyelids halfway—"I think she said this . . . *mail fraud?* Anyway, there she was, in the hollow of the law's hand, so to speak. Rather than being squeezed, she became an informer. She works for the DEA, watching the coast."

"What's mail fraud?"

"Forgot to ask," de Gier said. "I think the post office here has its own inspection." He waved around him. "Free democracies are tricky places."

"This one has good roads," Grijpstra said. "I like that interstate. I tell you, if I ever get really distraught back home, I'll take that El Al plane out here again and rent one of these Ford products of yours and just *drive*."

"You'll fall asleep."

"I'll hire a beautiful lesbian lady driver."

"Aki won't duplicate." De Gier smiled. "So we're doing good." The smile thinned out. "Both you and I, being experienced interrogators, get through to subject. She tells all, including and up to how the DEA directs her to Jameson, Maine. She needs a job for a front and there's Beth looking for a compatible live-in waitress." De Gier tried a new configuration, Honey Bear dominated by the combined forces of Worcestershire and horseradish sauce. "The princess and her princess buy a CD player and listen to jazz trumpets for ever after."

They studied their menus.

Grijpstra looked over his. *"So what?"*

De Gier nodded. "We should play that. I've got it all on paper. I've been trying to learn but it's hard to transcribe Miles, he sounds incomprehensible at half time, you ever noticed that? The man is just too subtle. At half time that probably doubles. Now if you play Clifford Brown at half time nothing much changes. But all-enlightened practitioner Davis . . ."

"Yes. Yes."

"You listening?"

"Sure," Grijpstra said. "But I meant 'So what?'—not the tune, the question. So what if Aki tells us she's spying on us and that she loves us and won't tell so we tell her what we're doing here and she tells on us anyway? The foreigners she has nothing to do with anyway thrown out? The tricksters tricked?"

De Gier laughed.

Grijpstra shook a heavy head. "Not funny, Rinus."

"But we didn't tell her . . . No!" De Gier put his hand over his mouth. "You *did* tell her? About me and Lorraine? You didn't. Did you? Of course you did. She seduced you. Alone, shy, lonesome . . . oh, shit . . ."

Grijpstra grinned. "Scared you?"

"So you didn't tell her anything," de Gier said. "Okay, this is what I know. Aki and Lorraine were friendly. Sister biologists. They've been out kayaking on occasion, to hear the loons chant at daybreak. Has Aki missed Lorraine yet?"

"She didn't say so."

"So she may still think we're here for drugs." De Gier moved more bottles around. "I was smoking pot the night I pushed Lorraine. She gave it to me too. It came from Jeremy Island, it's all over the place there, hidden under trees mostly. The fishermen grow it."

"With the sheriff's blessing?"

"Of course," de Gier said. "Give and take. Yankees are like the Dutch—why fight if you can split the dollar mostly

JANWILLEM VAN DE WETERING

your way? But the homegrown stuff is hard work and doesn't compare in quality to what Hairy Harry is bringing in."

"Or doesn't bring in."

"What?"

Aki came to take their order. De Gier ordered crab rolls for both. "Aren't you lucky?" Aki said to Grijpstra. "You get to eat again and I rush straight back to work. Aren't we busy?" More fishermen were coming in, she had to hurry off.

"Didn't Aki tell you about the arrests near the Point?" Grijpstra asked.

"I heard," de Gier said. "You mean the DEA missing out on the truckers who came to pick up a ship's load of Jamaican or Guatemalan or some other top-quality pot, hidden here near the Point? I read about it. So what happened really?"

"Aki didn't tell you?" Grijpstra looked surprised. "I thought she told all."

"Not all." De Gier looked modest. "I'm not the fatherly type."

"I'm not sure about the details," Grijpstra said. "She said someone spotted the shipment from the air, so that was probably Ishmael. Her contact told her he saw stacks of bales, in camouflage-colored covers hidden on the shore somewhere near here. So Aki tells her secret employer, and the DEA tells Hairy Harry, as it's his turf. Hairy Harry and Billy Boy hide in the woods waiting for someone to pick up the consignment. The DEA is there too, eager pimply youths according to Aki, lots of them, hands on guns, but Hairy Harry, being the local warlord, is in charge."

"Oh dear," de Gier said.

"Right. An eighteen-wheeler backs up slowly into the glade, the driver and his mates jump out of the truck's cabin . . ."

". . . and before they can put their hands on the merchandise Hairy Harry is out there snapping on handcuffs." De Gier nodded wisely. "That's how it goes."

"Need to hear the rest of it?"

"If you please."

"So the truckers tell the judge they were parking the truck for lunch, and just as they were going to break out the hamburgers there's Bald Baby and they don't know why. How could they know there were bales of marijuana hidden in the bushes? 'Jeez, Judge . . . what kind of a place is this Maine anyway?' "

"And the judge says he regrets the inconvenience caused to these nice out-of-state truck drivers trying to have lunch at the wayside."

"Never underestimate local authority's expertise at exploiting its area."

"Hairy Harry did lose his shipment, though," de Gier said. "He must have been saddened. But what the hell, you lose ten percent, ninety percent is still millions."

Aki brought the crab rolls, a foot long, well filled.

Grijpstra ate. "You know the biggest-size crab roll in Holland now?" He held his thumb and index finger two inches apart. "Costs a day's wage too." He leaned over. "About this case of yours. *Know your enemy.* Remember the stratagem? Say I used that on Aki, flipped into her mind. Say we can use the trick on the others too. Aki told me that Flash and Bad George are musical, Flash on the tuba, Bad George on the fiddle. School-band days. A musical get-together?"

De Gier thought that was funny. He choked on his crab roll.

Grijpstra waited. "Okay? Aki said Ishmael plays piano."

"A faulty upright," de Gier said, still smiling in spite of his pains. "We tried 'St. Louis Blues' together. I wailed. He pecked. But Flash Farnsworth on the tuba?" De Gier choked again. Grijpstra, eyes closed, chewing and smiling, ignored the disturbance.

"I'm okay now," de Gier said.

Grijpstra swallowed. "Here is what we do. I want you to tell Flash and Bad George that you're not going through with this extortion nonsense, you want to get that bullshit out of the way. That you like them, and that dumb dog is okay too, that you don't want them to think they have something on you. You can pay them something for expenses, hold out a little more for later."

De Gier nodded. "Fine."

"You offer a get-together party."

"Do some bonding?" de Gier asked.

"Force a bit of a showdown," Grijpstra said. "We're running out of time. Aki was over at Lorraine's quite a lot?"

"Yes." De Gier nodded.

"And she could go again any time soon," Grijpstra said, "and then raise the alarm." He ruefully contemplated his empty plate.

"Look," de Gier said, shifting about on his chair a bit, "I know what you're getting at—create some easy atmosphere, get somebody to talk so that we can find out where the body is. I don't care, of course, and you're in charge, but what do you think those jokers, Flash and Bad George, would do if they got irritable, or downright angry?"

"Let's see now," Grijpstra said. "They might dig up the body and show it around."

"Which makes them accessories," de Gier said. "Whatever way they present their case, either they buried Lorraine themselves or they watched me do it. So why haven't they told? Because they mean to suck me dry? That's another charge."

"So they won't do that," Grijpstra said. "They would rather drop a hint. Sheriff finds Lorraine's remains. After that the finger points. At who? At *you*."

"Because of the autopsy," de Gier said, "coroner concludes that body was abused, causing miscarriage . . ."

"No evidence for Harry to link killer and corpse," Grijpstra said. "Flash and Bad George know that too. Nothing but vague conjecture . . . slippery stuff." He pushed his chair back. He held his head to the side. He dropped his voice. "But rattling little guys with loving kindness may be a good way to find Snow White."

De Gier looked nervous. "You sure that's the way to play this?"

"I don't want to play at all," Grijpstra said, "but I'm in this now. They have nothing on you. Nobody saw you kick the woman. I don't want you paying off hoodlums."

De Gier smiled. "Hoodlums—Flash and Bad George? I don't really mind giving them money. They can fix up their tub."

"They won't get greedy and keep hounding you for more?"

"Yes," de Gier nodded. "There's that too."

"For sure there's that too," Grijpstra said. "And maybe that's still not the point. You want to find out if you did what it seems you did. You can't accept that in yourself. You don't really believe it. Without the body you'll never know."

"I can't live with this," de Gier said. "You know that, don't you?"

"What if you have to?"

De Gier shook his head. "Maybe I could accept it in you. My best friend turns out to be a killer, so? Man has to use whatever happens to be around." He sucked in his cheeks, raised his upper lip, and imitated the commissaris's slightly shrill voice. "Gentlemen, please remember: You can only use people the way they come, not the way you'd like them to come."

"So you're a user now too?" Grijpstra laughed, then looked serious. "You would still want me for a friend even if I kicked Nellie down her new oak stairs?"

"You'd be sorry, wouldn't you?" de Gier asked.

"Are *you* sorry?"

"Yes," de Gier said. "I'll never drink or do dope again."

"Try a year."

"Ever," de Gier said. "It releases the wrong demons."

"Maybe you have to accept them in yourself."

"And keep calling you to put them back in their cages?"

"Do what you have to do," Grijpstra said. "See if I care. I don't drink either now. We can be boring together."

"This may be another possible aspect of the human predicament in all its horrifying glory," de Gier said. "A problem you become aware of when it is too late. I could be programmed not to be able to handle liquor, genetically burdened with the chronic and incurable disease alcoholism, unaware of evil powers that control me."

"We'd have to go by the symptoms first," Grijpstra said. "We haven't even determined whether you pushed or kicked the missing person. We haven't got anywhere. You're no help either. You didn't even tell me what you knew about Aki working for the DEA here." He gestured. "I know, I know, that would lead to Hairy Harry and you claim the sheriff has nothing to do with this, all I have to find is the body. But that sheriff decided to kill me the minute he set eyes on me."

By then they were out of the restaurant. De Gier opened the car door for Grijpstra, gently pushed him inside.

Grijpstra sat, watching trees flash by. "I don't need this, Rinus. Hairy Harry's business interferes with what you got me out here for. There's more going on here than your personality disorder. It's like everything I ever try to do: In order to fix Nellie's faucet you have to clean out the shed to find the clamp."

De Gier parked the car, opened Grijpstra's door, pulled Grijpstra out, held him by the shoulders, aimed him at the Point's dock.

"Sheriff Hairy Harry complicates my life," Grijpstra said.

De Gier shoved gently.

Grijpstra walked slowly down the path, between junipers and a picket fence covered with flowering vines.

"Nothing changes," Grijpstra said. "You're still Mr. Hot Shit. I can't stand you as a client. You should be helping out. You're another complication."

"Me?" de Gier asked. "I'm the loser here. I'm underfoot? How can I possibly ever get in your way?"

Grijpstra nodded energetically. "I keep tripping over you. Like over the sheriff. Hairy Harry's heavy hand is all over these islands. I'll have to fix you fuckers."

De Gier rowed. Grijpstra sat on the dinghy's back seat. There was no wind and the little boat skimmed along quietly, driven by de Gier's long strokes. A loon floated by, chuckling dreamily, its long head pointed down. Late sunlight lit up white polka dots on the bird's wings. The loon lifted its wings briefly, showing its startling white chest.

"Aki calls it the magic bird of Maine," Grijpstra said.

De Gier leaned on his oars for a moment. "You did like Aki, you got that much . . ."

Grijpstra nodded. "When fate throws strangers together, briefly . . ."

De Gier grunted agreement.

Grijpstra put out his hands in enthusiasm. "You know, I often think, that must be heaven: brief relationships between sympathetic strangers, no hassle, no sex. Who needs sex? I'm too old." He patted his belly. "You don't want to inflict ugliness on a partner. No, just drive up and down that interstate and eat mussels, or what we had at that oyster restaurant in Boston, quahogs? Stuffed . . ."

"That's nice. . . ."

"Know what we did afterward? In the Parker House suite? Aki sat in her huge bed, and I sat in my huge bed, and the waiters rolled in all that room service. Pirouetting, graceful chaps, lifting huge silver lids off huge silver dishes. . . ."

"But you just had those quahogs," de Gier said. "What is this? The final feast? You eat instead of . . ."

"No, no. We did this right. We went to another hotel in between, with a bar and a turning platform, big black man on piano, same hair as your friend Flash but more tufted up, they did that Don Cherry thing you like, a Thelonious theme with percussion, no trumpet, a cello instead, doing both rhythm and solo. What is it called now?" Grijpstra touched his knee with a knuckle. "'Bemsha Swing!'"

". . . cello didn't get squeaky?"

". . . sleeping apart together. That's the way to really partake of true intimacy." Grijpstra pointed a finger. "Some think they always have to go the whole way . . . no . . . the cello was fine. . . ."

"Why did you take a suite in that hotel?" de Gier asked. "Weren't there any rooms?"

"Why did you buy this two-thousand-dollar dinghy?" Grijpstra asked. "Aki and I passed a marina. Used dories on sale. Good solid fiberglass. Cheap enough too."

"A handcrafted cedar dinghy weighing under sixty pounds is more fun."

"True," Grijpstra said.

"I was just curious, Henk. I'm happy for you. I don't care what you spend, the more the better." De Gier frowned. "It's hard to think of things sometimes, expensive things, I mean. Mostly you don't need them."

"You could be sailing the *Macho Bandido,*" Grijpstra said. "But you don't want the hassle. I've mostly run out of things to spend money on too. Nellie didn't even have a mortgage. Her house is just perfect now. I had to break out a wall to fit the new TV in but that was the last luxury she wanted."

"Spending is easier when you travel," de Gier said, "but I think I'm about done with that now. If you can clear this up I might go back with you."

"Help me out with the agency?"

"I'm open to offers."

"What if we don't clear this up?"

De Gier pulled on the oars again. He was shaking his head.

Chapter 11

Grijpstra's nap lasted till late evening. He walked along the island's little beaches after that, and set off a bear alarm, a nylon line strung between large boulders, that brought out de Gier.

"Nice here," de Gier said, putting his camera away. So it was, Grijpstra thought. Moonlight on a calm sea, the never-figure-out-able zillion stars everywhere, seals assuming their tail-up, head-up banana postures on rocks being bared by low tide, a quiet ripple further along, cut, de Gier claimed, by a curious dolphin's dorsal fin.

"Very nice," Grijpstra agreed. "Proves things are okay maybe. Here, for instance."

"But there are lots of Heres. Most Heres are *bad*."

"Bad enough to row away from forever?"

"But if I row out of Here altogether," de Gier said, "no bad Here is anywhere."

Grijpstra frowned.

"It goes further than that," de Gier said. "It includes you too. The world needs me to be. *You* need me to be."

"If you're not here, none of any possible Heres are here?" Grijpstra asked. "You know that's all bullshit, don't you? *I'll* still be here. Eating hundred-dollar crab rolls in Amsterdam and watching people starve in the Here-Too places that the news is always checking out for dying babies."

"Switch off your TV," de Gier said, "then use your unlimited Diners Club credit card and spend the night harmonizing your spirit with the likes of Aki."

"Just one night," Grijpstra said. "One night off doesn't mean that I don't suffer the human problem. Don't get so smart, Rinus."

"Now that we're on the subject again"—de Gier raised an eyebrow—"did anything between you and Aki, eh . . ."

"No," Grijpstra said.

"Look," de Gier said. "Maybe we don't agree philosophically but we can still be friends. Tell me. I've got this reputation but I don't really ever know how to be with women. It's very complicated. There's this theory that homosexuality is linked to being immature, and you must have done your fatherly/friendly thing again. You're *sure* nothing happened?"

They were back in the pagoda, drinking Louisiana coffee and chicory on the second floor's gallery. "This coffee is good and strong," Grijpstra said. "Most coffee here is weak."

"Regular American coffee is weak so that the citizens can drink it all day," de Gier lectured. "Because the country is worked by robots now. There's nothing more to do. Humans pour coffee into the great gap of free time. Drinking thirty cups a day is something to do."

Grijpstra glared.

"I'm sorry," de Gier said. "I thought you wanted me to explain America."

"Bah," Grijpstra said.

"But you already know it all," de Gier said. "Aki explained local degeneration. Where? In bed?"

Grijpstra smiled. "In your Ford product, on the way back from Boston. Hawaiian degeneration only. She was upset about the exhibition of Hawaiian historical art she saw in Boston while I was at the bank getting dollars for guilders. The paintings showed what the pre-Coca-Cola-and-hamburger era must have been like."

"Pre-Captain Cook-y scenes by a cookie-tin artist?"

"You know you amaze me?" Grijpstra asked. "You're the accused here. How can you try to be witty?"

"I forget sometimes," de Gier said. "Don't remind me. Go on. We're in Hawaii by Norman Rockwell."

"Norman Rockwell is no cookie-box-top-artist."

"I'm sorry."

"Okay." Grijpstra relayed the Hawaiian original scene with wide hand strokes. "Natural perfection . . . paradise . . . beaches before the oil slick . . . unsprayed fruit trees . . . straw-roofed houses with no broken toys in the yard . . .

outrigger sailboats with no two-stroke outboards . . . beautiful priestesses swaying around the king . . . climate . . ."

"There must still be climate."

"Bad smog in Honolulu now," Grijpstra said.

De Gier pointed at the ocean, clearly visible up till the horizon. "Nothing here."

There was the sudden roar of twin outboards. The boat at the end of a widening wake showed no navigation lights. "Probably Hairy Harry," de Gier said. "I often hear him. He must have brought in another shipment last week. He was ferrying like crazy. He kept going out, must have been a South American vessel off the coast somewhere."

"Does he ever see you?"

"We wave."

"Ignorance breeds fear," Grijpstra said. "You have no good reason to be here. He must be dreaming up theories."

"If I were Hairy Harry," de Gier said, "I would theorize that we represent a potential competitive supplier, out of Suriname or another former Dutch colony, St. Maarten maybe, St. Eustatius, there are all those places. We're checking out the scene and will be butting in soon."

"And we're not black or Latino," Grijpstra said. "We're his own kind, white repressed puritan Protestants, his own special brand of evil, a perfect match. Must be upsetting to Hairy Harry."

"Nellie convert you to Christianity?" de Gier asked. "I'd like to be Catholic sometimes. There was an article in the *Police Gazette* I studied once, about how the Catholics die more easily." De Gier shook his head. "It even showed statistics."

"Hairy Harry blundering between fear and desire, same way as us." Grijpstra looked across the pagoda's gallery at the empty expanse ahead, streaked by long lines of slowly moving riptides that lit up white in the moonlight. "Could there be competition here? The last inadequately patrolled United States coastal waters?"

"There's the Coast Guard," de Gier said. "They have huge helicopters. One of them landed on Jeremy Island. There, see the white pines on the west side, there's a flat area there. The pilots like that spot. This big ponderous giant chopper sets herself down and opens her slit and out pop five fat babies in orange zipper suits. The littlest carries the biggest basket and it's filled with burgers and fries and chips and cheezies and fritters and jerkies and any soda-pop known to modern man. The zipper suits sit around the basket and grab and tear and crackle and bubble it all inside and slip back into the slit and off they go again. If they'd just walked inland a few yards or so they would have seen pot plants everywhere."

"Leave a mess, these grabbers and tearers and cracklers and bubblers?"

"Those zipper suits don't bend easily," de Gier said. "Hard to pick up things that get scattered about.

"Lorraine used to." De Gier looked guilty. "She couldn't stand litter. She'd kayak out of her way for miles to pick up a can glittering on a beach, or a bit of silver paper.

She'd collect everything else too. She always carried garbage bags to stow things away in."

"Right," Grijpstra said.

They sat quietly. Bats squeaked. Crickets set up a wave of silver sound that subsided slowly. A sea duck quacked.

"Let me see if I got this now," Grijpstra said. "Fishermen grow marijuana on the islands; the sheriff condones that provided nobody squeals about what he is bringing in in bulk from abroad. Bildah Farnsworth builds houses for part payment in unregistered cash. Aki reluctantly spies on behalf of pimply-faced DEAers but she did her job the other day so she can relax now. Hairy Harry keeps going."

"Hairy Harry has got it made," de Gier said.

"Except for the usual money problem," Grijpstra said. "He launders one hundred thousand dollars via his house but the flow keeps flowing. Every time he fills up an eighteen-wheel truck he makes . . . what . . . ?"

"Too much," de Gier said. "Hairy Harry is exceptional. He did manage to sink some of his loot into his house. Most people here are too tight for that. Nobody here likes to show wealth. All Billy Boy ever spends is enough to buy new tires for the little old truck he keeps behind his trailer."

"Too much cash for the sheriff to ever get rid of," Grijpstra said. "Twice too much when he brings in cocaine."

"Keeps adding up," de Gier said. "Drug dealers who have it together eventually tend to choke on their millions." He touched Grijpstra's hand. "A well-known problem."

"The sheriff must have bad dreams," Grijpstra said. "I have a new nightmare now—I'm wading through bank-notes, getting in deeper slowly. A new kind of sinking dream. Unnerving."

"With me it's stuff," de Gier said. "I have all these vehicles and boats and airplanes and I forget where I leave them and they have to get their oil changed. Embarrassment of riches, here. . . ." De Gier brightened up. "I have another example, relevant to our case. Did you see that yacht in Jameson Harbor? The *Macho Bandido?* Some foreign alleged cocaine exporter bought it at the boat show in Portland. Paid cash. A million, a million and a half. Computerized, a cabin you can't imagine. The vessel was built somewhere around here. There are some of the best boat builders in the world on the New England coast. Maybe forty men worked on that yacht, all experts, so this guy plunks down his bag of soiled bank notes and sails away with his dopey friends, *muy macho,* 'to explore the Maine coast.' Hard to believe that they made it all the way up here. Very treacherous coast, you know." He waved at the view. "Looks fine, eh? Calm sea, lovely islands, but you have to watch it. People don't realize that."

"My dear chap," Grijpstra said. "The currents, the tides, the shoals, the waves, the goddamn wildlife that clowns around . . ."

"Ah yes," de Gier said. "Sorry, Henk. So this dealer and his mates eventually bungle the yacht into the harbor here . . . three fellows and a woman. They hang around for a bit, don't even have enough sense to ask if they can use a mooring. Just dump the anchor on a short cable that keeps dragging the boat's nose down at high tide. Do some partying aboard, finally go ashore in their brand new rubber boat, use their cellular phone to get a rental company to drop off a Cadillac, have themselves chauffeured away. Left the rubber boat, left the yacht, glad to be rid of it probably. They must have had some scary moments out on the Bay of Fundy—they took off in the car, that's a week ago, and haven't been seen since."

"I saw *Macho Bandido*," Grijpstra said, "from the restaurant. It was at a mooring and Little Max was swabbing the deck. The jib used to be all screwed up on that line that connects the bow sprit to the mast top. It looks nice now."

De Gier laughed. "Of course, the new owners take good care of it. The fishermen wanted to lengthen that anchor cable but Hairy Harry wouldn't let them. Some fishermen were talking on the radio just now. Last night, somehow, that cable managed to snap and the yacht managed to float out to sea where Harry happened to be, out on his own time, on a powerboat privately owned by Bildah Farnsworth, who happened to be on his boat too, and together they salvaged an abandoned vessel."

"And they get to keep a million dollars' worth of yacht?"

"Yessir," de Gier said. "Such is the law. It's also the law of life. Once you're rich you get to have it all. Once you're in the middle you dwindle. Once you're poor you lose what's left."

"Four people on *Macho Bandido* originally?"

"I never saw any of them," de Gier said. "The limo picked them up at night, Beth saw it leave. Aki noticed the crew a few times earlier, grocery shopping, having a meal at the restaurant. Aki said they were well-groomed Latino types and the woman looked like a white model out of *Vogue*."

Grijpstra's eyes didn't seem to be focusing.

"You okay?" de Gier asked.

"Too much going on here," Grijpstra said. He checked his watch. "Mind if I borrow the dinghy and the Ford product?"

"Not much to do in Jameson at midnight," de Gier said.

"And some quarters."

"Nellie'll be asleep."

"No," Grijpstra said. "It'll be six A.M. in Amsterdam. I promised I would phone early mornings.

Chapter 12

"Aren't you getting tired listening to this?" Katrien asked, about to play the tape again. "This must be the fourth time. Doesn't it get repetitive?"

The commissaris sat in the bath, slowly hitting the water's surface with his flat hands. *Smick, smeck.*

"But that's what detectives do," Katrien said, "isn't it? Go through the same thing again and again?"

"Not unless they're dense," the commissaris said. "But I wasn't there, Katrien, and I can't ask direct questions." He laughed. "But Grijpstra is answering them anyway." He looked up. "Don't you think?"

"Playing games again," Katrien said. "Who is dense here, Jan? Don't you know that Grijpstra is talking to you? He would never report to Nellie. She says so. He might tell her afterward but not while the case is going on." She bent over and squeezed her husband's hand. "Not like you."

"So he knows I'm listening in?"

"Of course."

"But he isn't looking for guidance?"

"Of course he is, Jan."

"Nah," the commissaris said. He pushed a button in the air. "Would you mind?"

The tape ran. "HenkieLuvvie," Nellie said, "listen, really, I don't mind, but we must be honest with each other. Just tell me about this hula hoop woman—Akipappapalo, is it? Tell me, what did you guys do that night in Boston?"

"Nellie, please," Grijpstra said. "I needed information. The woman is a dyke, I'm an old fat guy now. What could have happened?"

"Did you have separate rooms?"

The commissaris made his finger spin a circle in air. Katrien fast-forwarded the tape. "Birds," Grijpstra said, "ravens, they still have ravens here, and eagles, with a six-foot wingspan. They must have pulled Beth's father out of his Packard . . ."

The commissaris waved imperiously. The recorder clicked off. "That's it," the commissaris said, "that's what Grijpstra has to follow up on. See what I mean? If only I could tell him. And it's so easy. He has that Ishmael, the pilot with his aircraft." He began to hit the bathwater again. *Smick. Smeck.*

"Don't do that," Katrien said. "You can be very irritating, Jan. I've just sponged the floor."

Smick. Smack.

"I'll turn on the cold water."

"De Gier would catch on," the commissaris said, "but he's into philosophy again. Clogs his mind. And Grijpstra is slow, *slow.*"

"You think de Gier will kill himself once he's sure he really kicked a pregnant woman to death?" Katrien asked as she helped the commissaris to get out of his bath.

The commissaris kept shaking his head.

"Jan! You have arthritis, not Parkinson's."

"Hmmm?"

"Will de Gier kill himself?"

"If subjects keep talking about it they may do it in the end," the commissaris said. "There's some conclusive statistical evidence I believe."

"Oh dear . . ." She dropped the towel.

"Like Jeremy," the commissaris said. "I like that. Once the situation is terminal, once *I* decide the situation is terminal, not some goddamn doctor, eh?" He nestled into the towel that she held up again. "And then, on that mysterious coast, where everything still happens, the last unpolluted water on earth, with loons escorting the boat, and an eagle above me, Katrien, to row myself into nothing at all, some quiet spot between ledges, behind a hilly island with dead trees on it, and cormorants in the branches, drying their spread-out wings . . ."

"And then the angel comes down and gently teleports you through Limbo but you manage to withstand all self-seeking temptations until you change into pure light?"

Katrien asked, rubbing him dry. "You'd have to use a gun. You don't just evaporate, you know. A gun is messy."

"I can buy a gun there," the commissaris said. "On Main Street. Perkins' Sports Store. America recognizes a man's right to carry arms."

"I was talking about de Gier," Katrien said.

He kissed her. "The ego tends to discuss itself, Katrien."

Chapter 13

There were ravens in the sky around the Tailorcraft, circling and soaring in quiet splendor, not going down to check out carrion below.

"The gulls?" Grijpstra asked.

Ishmael handled his controls obediently, making the little plane follow two black-winged gulls. The birds weren't scavenging but were picking up mussels, dropping them to break their shells to get at the juicy meat inside.

Tension rose as Ishmael spotted an eagle, and managed to fly alongside the huge bird for a while. The eagle majestically dipped and raised its wings, showing the large white finger feathers at their ends. The eagle led the plane to a fish-filled cove where it harassed a smaller bird, an osprey, until the fish hawk dropped the mackerel it had just grabbed and the eagle caught the shiny prey neatly.

"Nothing dead here," Ishmael said. "Didn't you say

that your dead object had to be fairly close to Squid Island? Okay if I turn back a bit again?"

Grijpstra saw Squid Island below, Bar Island next to it, and then Jeremy's island, with the remains of a cabin and what looked like broken sun panels in a frame on posts. Ishmael circled slowly. "Jeremy had set up his own electricity source. Got himself a computer and a printer."

"Writing something?" Grijpstra asked.

"I found a title and some disconnected notes."

"What was the title?"

"*AfterZen,*" Ishmael said. "Jeremy studied Buddhism once but he said you don't carry a boat after it has taken you to the other shore."

"Clever hermit," Grijpstra said. "Now, if local people were burying a corpse, and they didn't have much time, you think they would dig deep?"

Ishmael thought so. A shallow grave wouldn't just attract birds, but animals as well. Raccoons are good diggers. "If it were me I would dig down six feet, and top it with some good-sized rocks."

"But doesn't that take time?"

"Maybe not so much time. We're all part-time clammers here. Everybody keeps equipment for digging clams on their boats."

The plane was circling Bar Island.

"Now what were we looking for again?" Ishmael asked. "Something dead, you said? Something human?"

Grijpstra mumbled.

JANWILLEM VAN DE WETERING

"Anyone I know?"

Grijpstra was looking at Bar Island.

"I would have noticed," Ishmael said. "I'm up here a lot of the time. If there's any carrion, I see the birds eat it. There may be dead seals on the rocks, or dolphins, or pilot whales. Could be in the woods, a deer, or a moose. I always fly low to check it out. One never knows. I've found backpackers needing bug spray, fugitives in search of food, crazed veterans who've got to be told the war is over."

"You did that?" Grijpstra asked.

"Sure."

"You're your brother's keeper?"

"I hardly know my brother," Ishmael said. "It's the frustrated family thing, I think. One tends to replace unlovable loved ones by perfect strangers."

There seemed nothing out of the way below, except perhaps de Gier, who was out with his trusty Nikon, walking around on Squid Island's shore.

"Looking for Mr. Bear again," Ishmael said. He had seen Mr. Bear, an impressive black-and-brown specimen, clambering ashore near the Point at daybreak. Hairy Harry and Billy Boy were always looking for Mr. Bear too. Mr. Bear and Hairy Harry were the same size but Mr. Bear had hair all over. Mr. Bear was Hairy Harry's nemesis. Ishmael thought Mr. Bear inhabited Jeremy Island. Jeremy had said he had met sleepy bears wandering around his island on unseasonably warm winter days when they'd wake up and take the air before turning in again. In summer they were more likely to roam a large area.

"What else do you have here?" Grijpstra asked. "Wolves?"

"No," Ishmael said, "only coyotes. You can hear them howl when the moon is full or when the fire engine is testing out its siren in Jameson."

Grijpstra was looking down at Bar Island. He pointed. "Like that maybe?"

Ishmael said that coyotes were a bit bigger and tan colored. "That's Kathy Two coming back from her walk. The old junker must be close." Ishmael located the *Kathy Three*, anchored in a cove near the Point. "Flash must have put the dog ashore." Ishmael chuckled. "Kathy Two likes to call on Lorraine."

He pointed at the cabin cruiser. "Doing some work for a change, fishing for dinner."

Flash and Dad George, on folding chairs, feet on the railing, phallically raised their rods to greet the airplane.

Grijpstra thought it was interesting that a man would believe that a small woolly dog was his mother. Ishmael thought it was funny too but he had known Kathy One and there was a kind of everlasting indignation in the woman that this dog showed too—the same defiant attitude toward a universe created for the sole purpose of annoying her.

"And another thing," Ishmael said, "when Kathy Two is all done for the day and does her summing-up rumination on the boat's bow . . . the way she sits there, with her long tufted ears stuck out sideways, like braids on a Passamaquoddy woman—Flash's mother was part Native American, I'll have you know—and the face a little forward, that's Kathy One all right."

"Woman comes back as dog," Grijpstra said.

"There couldn't be no such thing," Ishmael agreed.

The Tailorcraft fluttered back to sea after weaving its goodbyes around the old cruiser.

"Old tub is ready to sink. Would fill up overnight if they didn't keep two bilge pumps going, which exhausts their batteries, and they're always short of fuel to regenerate them."

"So what if she sinks?" Grijpstra asked, "What happens to her proud owners?"

"Their type doesn't take well to handouts," Ishmael said.

"Then what?"

"Take handouts, what else?" Ishmael asked. "Food stamps for dog food. Public assistance check for booze. Housing Authority for rent."

"Then what?"

"More loss of self-esteem in the homeless shelter. Drunken driving in stolen cars. The judge will make them watch bad news in jail."

"Can that boat be repaired?"

"No," Ishmael said, "but money could buy them something better."

"Plenty of cash around here," Grijpstra said.

"All they have to do is find it," Ishmael said.

Now that the quest for corpse-eating birds had led nowhere Ishmael steered further out. *Macho Bandido* was sailing a few miles offshore, close to the wind, looking good and trim. So was the captain, a dapper little man in a blue blazer and white slacks, and a hat with a gold-braided visor.

"Bildah Farnsworth," Ishmael said, making the Tailorcraft dip its wings. Bildah waved. Hairy Harry's bald pointed skull shone in the bright sunlight. Obscenely, Grijpstra thought.

"Rubbed himself with sun-blocking oil," Ishmael said. "All that bald skin might burn badly in this weather."

The sheriff, reading the commentary in the sky, flashed a glimmering fist. The Tailorcraft, startled, veered back to the coast.

"Not so friendly now," Grijpstra said, looking back at the white sailboat, dainty now in the distance. He shook his head. "That sheriff is bad."

"Badly blissful at times," Ishmael said.

Grijpstra thought that was a contradiction in terms. A crime is a violation of a social law, aiming to diminish the common good. A criminal, damaging the well-being of the tribe to which he belongs, especially when he is chosen to protect the tribe's good, feels guilty. Guilt and happiness are opposite feelings and cannot go together. He explained as much.

Ishmael explained differently. Bad bliss comes about by

outsmarting tribal pressure. "Bildah Farnsworth and Hairy Harry are good at that."

Grijpstra grunted.

"I'm surprised you're small-minded," Ishmael said.

"There's good," Grijpstra said, "there's bad."

Ishmael shook his head. "We made that up ourselves. How about supposing there's neither? There's having a good time, though, but who dares to have it? Maybe Hairy Harry does." Ishmael narrowed his eyes wishfully while he poked Grijpstra's chest. "Let me tell you. There's a lake here, inland a bit. Few people can find it but it's easy to spot from the sky. A perfectly round lake, great for racing. There was a big marijuana plantation close by owned by out-of-county folks who Harry busted. One of the spoils was an antique speedboat with a racing engine.

"There she is," Ishmael said.

The Tailorcraft had reached the inland lake. The speedboat was still there, wrecked on rocks. "Silly Billy Boy did that," Ishmael said. "Billy Boy isn't very good with boats. Billy Boy isn't good at being happy. Hairy Harry is better. Hairy Harry is also a better boater. That day when I was flying across the lake he was zipping about at full speed, one happy sheriff in the smoothest of antique glorious speedboats, and behind him, water skiing, was . . ."

Ishmael turned to Grijpstra. "Can you hear me, Krip?"

"Yes."

"Engine not too noisy?"

"No."

". . . was a goddess, a naked goddess. The goddess was happy too."

"Good," Grijpstra said.

Ishmael's smile was crafty. "Kripstra, would you like to know who that honey-skinned long-legged raven-haired tumbly-titted goddess might have been?"

"Not Aki," Grijpstra said. "Not even when you say so. Okay?"

Ishmael patted Grijpstra's shoulder. "Just trying to make a point, Krip." He winked. "To myself maybe. I don't like to take sides. There aren't any, you know."

They flew home, Ishmael quietly, Grijpstra pensively for a while. To cheer himself Grijpstra watched for gasoline bubbles on the windscreen but the fuel pump worked fine now. They saw Ishmael's home on the way to Jameson's airstrip: the four-storied canning factory, no longer work- ing, close to the Point at the tip of the peninsula. They also saw Kathy Two, sniffing around a small weathered cabin on Bar Island.

"Looking for Lorraine," Ishmael said. The dog was standing up against the cabin's door.

"You know what twirling is?" Ishmael asked. He demonstrated the term, first making the plane gain height, then switching off the engine and twisting the Tailorcraft down. "Like a leaf in autumn?" Ishmael asked. "You like that?"

Grijpstra's eyes were closed but he heard Kathy Two bark furiously.

"It's like Lorraine is still alive," Ishmael said. "Like Kathy Two is disappointed that her friend isn't home."

Grijpstra groaned from an increasing depth of bottomless fear.

"If Lorraine," Ishmael was saying from a considerable distance, "were not alive, as you seem to think—since who were we looking for all morning, eh, Mister Detective?—Mrs. Farnsworth wouldn't bark, no sir, that dog would howl. . . ."

Grijpstra howled. The Tailorcraft was close to the water when Ishmael started the engine up again. The little plane straightened out easily and skimmed waves. "It's okay when there are waves," Ishmael said. "With waves you can see the surface. I lost a plane once when the water was still. You're supposed to buzz the water with your propeller, to see where it is so you won't hit it, but I hadn't learned that yet. The plane broke up when it dived and turned over.

"And you?"

"I broke my neck," Ishmael said, "but they can fix that now. They couldn't fix the plane, though."

Chapter 14

"No," Nellie said, half awake. "You've got his number? Shall I give it to you? Or are you out of quarters again? Shall I ask him to phone you? I don't want to do this anymore. I keep forgetting the questions. Are you all right? HenkieLuvvie, come back quickly now, stay away from that woman."

Grijpstra, leaning against Beth's Diner's wall, next to the pay phone, looked at Jameson Harbor. The fishing fleet was out. *Macho Bandido,* impeccable again, sails twirled and sheathed, tugged gently at its mooring. Bildah Farnsworth was on board, tipping back a shot glass, smacking his lips, swallowing, shivering, smiling. Hairy Harry, naked down to his gleaming bare belly button, was tearing off the top of another beer fresh from the cooler, watching rivulets of condensation run down the can's sides, pouring down foamy frothy cold . . . outdoing the commercials, Grijpstra thought. Grijpstra wanted to join Hairy Harry, have a beer himself, merge good and evil, go boating on the bay, tell jokes, laugh with his new friend, take Aki along, two charming and intelligent Akis—or three, one for Bildah too. Why all this animosity? Share a lovely planet in an unlimited universe, enjoy the short stay.

The pay phone rang. "Yessir," Grijpstra said, "did you just go to bed? Sorry to wake you up, sir."

"Adjutant," the commissaris said sleepily. "Oh, I beg your pardon, Henk, I mean, uh . . ."

"It's okay, sir," Grijpstra said. "You've been directing the case, I gather. How are your legs? I could have asked Nellie to phone you later but she hung up. Your legs bothering you, sir?"

"No," the commissaris said, "in fact, I'm planning to have a look at the Maine coast myself, but . . . no, please, Katrien, go back to bed. Sorry, Adjutant. . . ."

"Yessir. Any suggestions, sir?"

"Well, I'm sure you're doing an excellent job. I wish I could . . . no, please, Katrien, nobody is going anywhere yet. . . . Oh dear, now what have I done? Suggestions, Adjutant?"

"Yessir. Questions. Anything I should be doing now since I still can't find the body?"

"You're looking for the grave?"

"Maybe there isn't a grave," Grijpstra said. "Flash and Bad George don't strike me as too efficient."

"They did save your life, though."

"That was the dog."

"The famous dog." The commissaris chuckled. "Yes, I heard that."

"You had me taped, didn't you, sir?"

"Uh . . . yes . . . Katrien bought the machine, a recording gadget that clips to Nellie's phone. Very clear, Ad—Henk, wonderful what this new audio equipment can do. So, you think Flash and friend threw Lorraine's body overboard?"

"If it was Lorraine's body, sir."

"Good," the commissaris said. "That's good. You ascertained that another woman was missing?"

"Yes."

"Who?"

"I read all the recent newspapers kept at Beth's Diner, asked some questions. A sixteen-year-old reputedly ran away from abusive parents in Jameson, sir, but that missing person is overweight, with fat feet, sir."

"The corpse de Gier saw didn't have fat feet?"

"Slender feet, sir."

"But de Gier was incapable at the time."

"I think he did notice the feet on the body."

"So you believe he saw the dead body of a blond-haired woman with slender feet?"

"Yessir."

"Well, now," the commissaris said cheerfully. "De Gier wouldn't kick a pregnant woman. Is he still drinking now?"

"He says he will never drink again."

"Keep you company," the commissaris said. "He might not miss it. I've been cutting back myself. Drop of brandy with the coffee. So de Gier is not violent now, is he?"

"No, sir."

"And was he violent before the woman got hurt?"

"Yes," Grijpstra said.

"*What?* Are you sure, Adju—Henk? You mean to tell me that Rinus was habitually and physically abusing a girlfriend while under the influence of alcohol and/or drugs?"

"There was an incident involving firewood, sir. There's a big fireplace in the pagoda. When de Gier came here the nights were still cold. April, sir. Spring doesn't come until June. Firewood had been brought to Squid Island, cut and split, high-quality hardwood. Flash and Bad George do that sort of thing: caretaking. The firewood was nicely stacked. Sorted by size and color, an artistic job. They must have been paid by the hour. . . ."

"Don't tell me de Gier destroyed that beautiful firewood stack?"

"I'm afraid he did, sir. He kicked about half of it down the rocks. Got frustrated, he said, and the firewood was just sitting there."

"Did suspect tell you voluntarily?"

"No, sir. I was walking around the island and noticed the split logs lying on the beach so I reconstructed what must have happened."

"Did suspect lie? Tell you it blew down?"

"No, sir."

"What was de Gier frustrated about?"

"Well . . ."

"You know?"

"Yes," Grijpstra said. "It's the old thing again, his habitual ego problem. Wants to know what really goes on in life. He thought that the journey to New Guinea might help." Grijpstra chuckled. "Enlightenment under the banyan tree, sir."

"Where the shaman held court? Wasn't he initiated there?"

"Seems he flew when under the influence of an ingested plant," Grijpstra said. "Hallucinations. Being alone on the island here was supposed to have been the next stage but nothing much happened, except some highs on dope and recorded music."

"Miles Davis?"

"And Kentucky bourbon sipping whiskey, sir. But nothing to write home about."

"Classic Miles Davis or the funky electronic music?"

"In between, sir. The new quintet, with Wayne Shorter."

"Ah yes," the commissaris said. "Katrien has those records, she plays them for me sometimes. She has become quite the expert, her ear has widened, she says. She has been religiously studying jazz for years now."

"Transitions take time, sir."

"You like that funky stuff, Henk? That way-out percussion and the electric guitars and synthesizers going on and on? You're a sensitive drummer yourself."

"Acquired taste," Grijpstra said.

"And you acquired it?"

"Foley and Irving III are exceptionally good, I think, sir. As I was saying. So de Gier combined these highs thinking he'd get a super high . . ."

"That would set him free? And then nothing happened? He had to scatter firewood, kick women? That's sad . . . yes . . ."

"You still there, Henk?"

"Yessir."

"You do have to find the grave."

"I don't know how to, sir."

"Or find Lorraine."

"You still there, Henk?"

"Yes," Grijpstra said. "Yessir. I may have an idea. It'll be easy, all I need is some empty cans. . . .

"Tell me."

Grijpstra told the commissaris.

"You just thought of that? What triggered it?"

"Hairy Harry, sir. I just saw him toss his Heineken's can overboard, out of the *Macho Bandido*. Ishmael was telling me yesterday, as we were flying over the area looking for carrion birds, that Hairy Harry and the deputy, Billy Boy, weasel face I call him, go out shooting 'varmints' a lot. That's what they call wildlife. They have good equipment, infrared scoped rifles, and they keep killing beautiful birds."

"Oh dear," the commissaris said.

"I made some drawings, sir. Golden-eyes, mergansers—have you seen those here, with the russet tufts? And the little puffed-up fellows, buffleheads? And the loons?"

"I was there in the winter, Henk. I did see some ducks, but from a distance. I heard about the loons, eeric laughlike cry, I believe. Don't tell me you have the sheriff and the deputy sheriff shooting endangered species there?"

"Anything that flies," Grijpstra said. "Ishmael says there's an eagle missing too. He has been looking for the body. He did find two loons and fifty-two assorted ducks lined up on the rocks. Shot during breeding season."

"Ah . . . ," the commissaris said.

"Ishmael," Grijpstra said, "says the habit dates back to when poor British folks first settled the area here. Back in England they'd seen rich folks blast away at game all the time, so once they reached the promised land they all bought guns and blasted away too."

The line was quiet.

"Sir?"

"Hunt the human hunter," the commissaris said. "That's what I would like to do if I had my life to live over again. The predator's predator. Now there's a good home-made purpose, Grijpstra. Wouldn't that feel good? Protect the endangered species against the endangering species. To impress our ladies. Care to join me? Fancy coming home to

Nellie and when she says, 'How many?' you say, 'Got three of 'em, Nellie.' Wouldn't she be proud?"

"You're kidding, sir."

"Don't know if I am. Let me know what happens with your cans and things. . . . That'll be on Jeremy's island, you said? . . . Think a few good thoughts for me there, Henk. . . . There should still be a lot of Jeremy's spirit around on that blessed spot."

Chapter 15

Grijpstra located the grave
and the corpse. He also located Lorraine. He didn't locate
grave, corpse, and Lorraine at the same time.

Good luck comes to those who keep trying. The commissaris kept saying so during Grijpstra's long career as an
Amsterdam Municipal Police Murder Brigade detective.
The commissaris kept saying other things. "Doing what
you're doing now, Adjutant, is your present excuse for being
alive." Grijpstra hadn't quite gotten that at the time but he
was encouraged anyway, and pursued his activities, the endless search for the relevant detail that keeps a murder case, or
any other pursuit for that matter, up, no matter how totter-
ing. Up and about.

"Glad to see you're up and about, Adjutant," the com-

missaris would say when he saw Grijpstra striding through
the corridors of headquarters, a case file or object in hand.
Once there were two objects: Sten guns, as used by British
commandos. The weapons were found held by desiccated
hands in an Amsterdam basement. The theory was that the
uniformed mummies were the remains of liberation soldiers
who shot each other over treasure. No witnesses could be
produced. A probable date was set somewhere in the spring
of 1945. The bodies were discovered by masons in a next
door basement who ran into a bricked-up thruway twenty
years later. Grijpstra's theory said that British troops were
quartered in a house formerly occupied by German troops,
an SS detail, hunting the city for hidden Jews. Whenever
Jews were found, treasure showed up too. The SS men hid
their loot in the basement. They left it there as they fled. Two
British commandos discovered the cache. There seemed to
be quite a bit of value in the stacked foreign banknotes and
the jars containing jewels. Both soldiers realized simultane-
ously that all of a treasure is twice as much as half of a
treasure. They both carried murderous weapons. They both
had itchy trigger fingers.

"Glad to see you up and about, Adjutant," the commissaris had said briskly. A little later, in his office, he
approved of Grijpstra's theory. The soldiers' dried-out
corpses were delivered to the British embassy. There was no
further action. There was a grim detail, however. The treasure turned out to be worthless.

"Now," the commissaris had said at the time, "what if

instead of obsolete occupation money and colored glass we had a couple of million dollars here, and what if you and Sergeant de Gier had found those millions? We reflect on facts—long-gone owners, the loot is of criminal origin. And what if the society you serve has become chaotic? And what if authority has become corrupt? Would those millions become your ticket to freedom?"

"Would de Gier and I shoot each other?" Grijpstra asked.

The commissaris's phone was ringing. He picked it up, waving his trusted assistant away. "Yes, Katrien, of course I'll be home. What's for dinner? Kale? Mashed potatoes? No veal croquettes? But you promised."

It was nice to know, Adjutant Grijpstra would tell Sergeant de Gier, that a man of the commissaris's elevated status took an interest in lowly bunglers such as themselves and threw them outrageous ideas to chew on.

"And what's so elevated about the commissaris's status, Adjutant?" the sergeant would ask and Grijpstra wouldn't have much of an answer because he couldn't ever quite define why he admired his chief. The man's indifference? Or was there a better word? The man's curiosity? His willingness to probe taboos?

Adjutant and sergeant pursued the subject in the police headquarters' parking lot. The old watchman, in the city's uniform, sitting straight up on a stool, was enjoying the sun while listening in.

"He don't worry much," the old watchman had said,

pointing his grizzled head at the commissaris limping across to his privately owned ten-year-old dented Citroën convertible. "State would buy him one of them fancy limousines like the other bigwigs drive but he don't care to spend taxpayers' money on fancy new models."

The watchman, a constable now out of the force because of multiple shot wounds in both thighs, badly healed, didn't worry much himself, but he was always around, mathematically fitting the maximum number of cars into a fairly small space, always with freeway for emergency vehicles, giving them godspeed with his crooked smile as he held up traffic outside the gates as they flashed off, sirens screaming.

"Maybe that's it," Grijpstra said as he watched the former constable cheerfully swinging his crippled body about. "Not to worry while giving it all you can?"

De Gier smiled obediently. "Ah . . ."

"Not good enough, Sergeant?"

"Oh yes," de Gier had said. "Now tell me, Adjutant, what's this *it* we're supposed to give all to?"

"It ain't there," the former constable said. "If it was I couldn't serve it, right?"

Grijpstra made de Gier row him and two gray garbage bags filled with empty beer cans, candy bar wrappers, and other shiny garbage he had collected in Jameson earlier to Jeremy Island that night. Together they arranged the objects on a beach that would be visible from Bar Island.

"Can't have seen us," de Gier said. "It's too hazy for one thing, but I checked the weather report and the fog will burn off later today and the night will be clear. For another thing, Aki is working through the evening at the diner. If you're right, Lorraine will be hiding underground." De Gier laughed. "The trap is sprung, Henk."

"Good," Grijpstra said, surveying their work. "Sun rises in the east. East is over there. The first rays will light up the bait nicely. Subject of our search will see the mess. She, accompanied by Aki or not accompanied by Aki—that doesn't matter, we're not after Aki—will rush out and clean up. We grab subject. We solve our case."

"This must be too simple," de Gier said.

"I know," Grijpstra said. "I know I shouldn't discuss strategy with suspect . . ."

"Suspect may be crazy too . . ."

". . . with possibly psychopathic suspect . . ."

De Gier's flashed smile was pleasing

". . . but what else have we got?"

Grijpstra sat on a rock, embracing his knees. The gigantic luminous disk of a full moon was rising behind Squid Island, filling the sky with an eerie light that made firs and pines look like black fairy-tale cutouts. The momentarily tideless sea lapped the island gently. There was no wind and the peaceful whispering and rustling sounds behind them had to be made by animal life, equally impressed with the enchantment displayed all around. A loon, floating just off Jeremy Island, chuckled, and set off a choir of coyotes on the peninsula's point nearby. A soprano coyote yipped a few times and mezzo-sopranos set up rising howls for background. The mezzos warbled while the soprano sang. The chant rose for a while, faltered suddenly, then the sounds tapered off. A little tremulous yapping again . . . a long drawn-out musical sigh . . . the loon's chuckle.

Grijpstra applauded silently.

"Never heard coyotes this close." De Gier had found an egg-shaped boulder of his own to sit on. "They don't dare usually. Maybe they can sense we won't harm them. The sheriff and Billy Boy just love to shoot them."

"For the skins?"

"They fly coyote tails off their cars' antennas."

"Infrared scopes. Super rifles. Our brother sportsmen." Grijpstra growled. "I'd rather have them hunt us." He grinned. "Then turn on them."

"Defend the little bit of nature left," de Gier said. "I would like that too. The commissaris is right. The noble final venture. Exterminate the exterminators. . . . Henk?"

"Yes?"

"How can Lorraine pick up beer cans if I saw her corpse?"

"But you don't really believe that," Grijpstra said. "I'm here to prove the opposite. That's why you summoned me."

"No . . ."

"Okay," Grijpstra said. "Here's the other reason you summoned me—your emotional development was impeded, as you know . . ."

De Gier gaped. He raised his voice. "I know *what?*"

Grijpstra nodded. "The emotionally impeded need plenty of attention. Say I prove you did indeed kill Lorraine. Off you go, rowing into the horizon, in the two-thousand-dollar dinghy. Like the good hermit. Never to be seen again. And I'll be waving from the shore. Me, your alter ego, an essential segment of your final scene."

De Gier grinned. "Yes, Doctor Shrinkski."

Grijpstra grinned too.

De Gier's smile was ghoulish white in the moonlight.

Grijpstra shifted about on his rock. "The emotionally impeded live and die to impress the audience. But help is on the way—there's no need for you to emulate hermit Jeremy yet."

De Gier relaxed. "Just answer the question, Henk. How can Lorraine, dead, clean up this beach here?"

"Okay," Grijpstra said. "Why do I know that Lorraine is alive? Kathy Two is a smart dog. Smart enough to save my life. Smart enough to stay sane while living with the crazy little skippers. Explain this: Kathy Two keeps visiting Bar Island to bark at Lorraine's cabin, inviting her to come out and play."

"You told me that," de Gier said. "So where is Lorraine? Hidden and locked up by Flash and Bad George? Who's been feeding her all week?"

"Ever thought of tunnels?" Grijpstra asked.

"Tunnels," de Gier said. "Fascinating. You're supposed to get sucked into them after you have a heart attack. Then you come back and tell the folks back home what death is all about. We have Lorraine crawling back out of astral tunnels now?"

"Regular tunnels," Grijpstra said. "Tunnels of greed. Didn't you see that poster in the window at Perkins' Sports Store? Old-fashioned men in waistcoats leaning on their spades in front of a large shed with SILVER MINE written on the roof?"

"Wasn't that just another sham? Some rumor started to drive up the price of real estate?"

"The men in the waistcoats didn't know that yet. They dug lots of tunnels." Grijpstra patted his boulder. "Right here, these very islands, Jeremy, Squid, and Bar. All three of them have been tunneled for silver. I asked Beth. She showed me her family album. Her uncles got duped too. They borrowed money, bought the islands, went bankrupt, sold out."

"Flash and Bad George are feeding a chained-up Lorraine in an island tunnel?"

"Why assume willful constraint?" Grijpstra asked. "Why would she be kept there against her will?"

"She's cooperating?" de Gier asked. "She's out to get me? But we were having an affair, Henk. . . ."

"Did you humiliate Lorraine in any way?" Grijpstra asked.

De Gier jumped off his rock. He raised his voice. "We were having a good time together."

"Aha," Grijpstra said. "Overreacting, are we? Did you,

or did you not, put your loved one down in any way? Answer the question, suspect."

The lone coyote raised her voice too, howling sadly.

"Lorraine is a feminist," de Gier said, after the howl died down. "It's hard to share a good time with someone who keeps talking about Women and Earth, leaving no place for us suckers."

"No," Grijpstra said. "I've had that out with Nellie. Feminists believe in equality between sexes. You always do your superior thing, just for laughs, because you're not supposed to these days. That's not funny now. It aggravates the other party. Half of mankind, kept barefoot and pregnant in kitchens."

"Just kidding," de Gier said.

"You kidded with Lorraine?"

De Gier sat on his rock again.

"Yes?" Grijpstra asked.

"Yes," de Gier asked. "So I said something about women's tendency to invite abuse."

"And you were serious?"

"Takes two to tango," de Gier said.

"For God's sake," Grijpstra said. "What about my Nellie? Hey? And her Gerard? The pimp? You think she liked being in that position? You're not that stupid."

De Gier sat quietly.

"You tell Lorraine she invites abuse, and then you kick her down some cliffs."

De Gier lifted a hand. "Lorraine is dancing around in

the tunnels cackling with glee? Woman sets Man up for a change? All this was planned? And Aki is in this too? That's why she wanted to drive you to Boston? To find out how much, if any, you suspected? Aki and Lorraine sharing money extorted from me by Flash and Bad George?"

Grijpstra looked at the moon, smaller and higher now, but still luminous and powerful.

"You can't be right," de Gier said. "There's still the corpse Flash and Bad George showed me, and I recognize corpses, no matter how befuddled I get. But if this *is* revenge, then Aki is in it too. And Beth. Don't underestimate Beth. That dinner party she threw for you because you had such a good time with her lover, you think that little trip just happened?"

"Yes," Grijpstra said. "I had to change guilders into dollars and Aki wanted to go to Boston anyway to see the Hawaiian art exhibition. Beth was too busy to accompany Aki. You offered the Ford product. It all just happened."

"No foresight?"

"Hindsight," Grijpstra said. "Things happened and Aki happened right along."

"To test you?"

"Of course." Grijpstra smiled. "To test you through me. If I was an asshole too . . ."

"Then you would have shoved Aki down some rocks off the interstate's shoulder. . . ." De Gier dropped his head a little sideways. "Please . . ."

Grijpstra dropped his head a little sideways too. "Don't you see? Your general attitude toward Lorraine was abrasive, humiliating, arrogant. Aki and Beth back Lorraine. The idea was to punish men in general; you were the man in particular. Nobody knew how that was to come about, no plan had been discussed, and nothing would have happened if you hadn't been rude to Lorraine that evening, just as she was very susceptible . . . getting dark at that time . . . her period . . . very vulnerable, Rinus. You pushed, she fell, she bled, she was found by her friends . . ."

De Gier gestured defensively.

"Truth hurts," Grijpstra said. "I'm just showing you another side of the picture, a nasty side—your side was nothing to phone home about either. The locals need money for a new boat and here you are, incredibly rich, an outsider they can prey on. . . ."

"Flash came by this morning," de Gier said. "To ask about his outstanding bills. I told him I'd only pay reasonable rates for the use of his boat and his time, and something for Bad George, say five hundred dollars in all. He said that would be fine."

"No threats?" Grijpstra asked.

"No."

"No anger?"

"Flash seemed relieved."

"Where was Bad George?"

"He stayed on the boat."

"Did you ask Flash about the corpse?"

"No," de Gier said. "But that corpse exists. I *saw* it. A corpse with Lorraine's hair."

"Not her feet?"

"Maybe not her feet."

"There may be no grave," Grijpstra said. "But Aki is still involved and maybe Beth, and Flash wants to stay in with them. The corpse you saw was not Lorraine's."

"You can't be sure," de Gier said.

"Once we see a living Lorraine pick up beer cans right here in front of us, on this very beach," Grijpstra said, "we will be sure."

"You think that's about to happen?"

"I wouldn't be surprised."

"So there is no corpse?" de Gier asked. "I was seeing things that night? The evil blackmailers fooled me?"

"We're still theorizing," Grijpstra said. "You're a trained Murder Brigade detective. You claim to have seen a corpse, but you were also out of your mind. I'm proposing now that Lorraine is alive and that therefore there was no corpse."

"If Lorraine is alive," de Gier said, "she is hiding and Aki must be feeding her. There's still that university paper Lorraine is writing on loons. She wouldn't give up on that. Those two will be out loon viewing some mornings."

"Wouldn't you see them?"

"I haven't been getting up early much," de Gier said. "I should have. Best time of the day. . . .

"Drinking, smoking pot, playing CDs," Grijpstra said. "You're not getting any younger. A hermit needs his rest. So they know the spiritual seeker sleeps late?"

"We could make sure," de Gier said, as he rowed Grijpstra back to Squid Island. "If you're right, which you still may not be, Aki and Lorraine will be watching us."

"Here? But Squid Island is between Jeremy Island and Bar Island. They can't have seen us put out those cans and things."

"They could see us on Squid Island," de Gier said.

Later that night the sounds of jazz ballads composed by Miles Davis and Sonny Rollins floated from the pagoda, across the channel between Squid Island and nearby Jeremy Island. De Gier's tall silhouette and Grijpstra's plumper form were framed in the pagoda's brightly lit windows. The silhouettes appeared to be smoking pot, making exaggerated movements as they waved their reefers.

"I can feel binoculars aimed at us," Grijpstra said.

De Gier fanned his burning stash of marijuana, set on a plate. "The wind is their way. I think they will smell this."

"You think they're on the water somewhere, in their kayaks?" Grijpstra asked.

De Gier didn't think so. Lorraine didn't see too well in the dark. Grijpstra thought that was interesting. "Night blind?"

"Somewhat."

"Nellie can't see well in the dark either," Grijpstra said. "She has trouble gauging depth. The evening that

Lorraine came to see you she must have expected to stay the night."

"So?"

"That's why she was upset when you wouldn't let her, you clod," Grijpstra said, pointing an accusing finger. "Try to remember. It was getting dark when all this happened?"

"Yes."

"Nellie hates walking down steps in the dark. Aha." Grijpstra prodded de Gier's stomach. "Now, when you pushed her, could she have mistaken the rock she stood on for the top step of the stone stairs?"

"Yes."

"Good," Grijpstra said. "Better. So maybe you just put a hand on her, and as she was angry with you she stepped back, thinking there was a step there, but there wasn't. She fell, she badly scraped her skin, she bled. She shouted for help. You were listening to jazz, turning the volume up, you didn't hear her. Flash and Bad George arrived, they told you Lorraine was bleeding, in bad shape, you didn't even bother to check. Doing your shamanic shit with the record, you told Flash and George to take her to the doctor in Jameson. Lorraine got extremely *annoyed* with you."

"Didn't she overreact?" de Gier asked. "I mean, really. It was the wrong night for her to sleep over. It was my island. I do pay rent, you know. Am I right?"

Grijpstra laughed.

"What's funny?"

"That you're asking me about what is right."

They rowed back to Jeremy Island again, quietly, oars wrapped in towels so they wouldn't splash. De Gier remembered the detail from a boy's pirate book.

"Pirates have towels?" Grijpstra asked.

De Gier had also brought sleeping bags, coffee in a thermos, a jar of olives, peanut butter and hot sauce sandwiches.

"Pirates eat peanut butter and hot sauce?" Grijpstra asked.

De Gier set his alarm for four o'clock, daybreak. The avengers would be ready to catch Lorraine as soon as she beached her kayak, greedy to collect shiny trash, but first the avengers would rest. De Gier snored as soon as he had zipped himself into his sleeping bag. Grijpstra, slapping mosquitoes, wandered about the island. The sea was calm, the moon bright in a clear sky. Grijpstra rowed the dinghy, thinking bugs would bother him less on the water. A bald-headed harbor seal, taking a breather after a spell of night fishing, showed up too close to the dinghy and, in its hurry to get away, flopped over backward in fear. Grijpstra shushed the seal, and ravens, flapping between the islands' treetops, croaked warnings at the human intrusion. Another dark head floated close by, a woolly head. A woolly seal? There were probably different kinds of seals around. Grijpstra remembered de Gier talking about a gray seal, with a long head like a horse. This seal's head was round, with furry ears that stood up straight. Grijpstra marveled at the swimming animal's self-reliant composure. The day before, while

Grijpstra was sitting quietly below the pagoda, a large rabbit had calmly hopped by his feet. Rabbits, Grijpstra thought, have their separate reality. So would woolly headed round-eared seals. This one was steering a straight course for Jeremy Island. Grijpstra, curious, pulled on the dinghy's oars, quickly overtaking the animal. He reached Jeremy Island's beach, clambered out of the dinghy, half-pulled, half-carried it ashore, and hid it behind moss covered rocks. He turned to watch the round-eared woolly headed seal walk out of the water, change into the bear he had been from the start. Mr. Bear, a large purplish black male specimen, crashed about between bushes, then slowly eased away into what had to be a hole in the hillside. Once inside he grunted, sighed, began to gnaw on something.

A bone snapped.

Grijpstra hesitated. Maybe Mr. Bear was eating a deer. Deer could swim out to the islands, die, become carrion, attract scavengers. Bears can smell rotting bodies miles away. Grijpstra noticed a stench. The body had to have been buried there, and Mr. Bear had dug it up.

"Mr. Bear!"

Mr. Bear emerged from the hole, stood seven feet tall, wanted to know what he could do for Grijpstra.

Grijpstra was sorry, he couldn't let Mr. Bear eat Lorraine. Lorraine was evidence. The hole in the hillside was a tunnel. In the tunnel would be a grave, dug by Flash and Bad George.

"Mr. Bear!" Grijpstra shouted, hoping to wake de Gier

some few hundred yards away. Grijpstra thrashed the bushes with a branch he had picked up. The branch snapped. He picked up another. "Mr. Bear!"

Animals, when faced by humans, are supposed to turn and run. They're supposed to know the universal line of command. First there is the Lord of Creation, then there's the Little Lord of Creation presented with the universe and all things nonhuman that that universe contains. Mr. Bear should present himself to serve the Little Lord. But Mr. Bear hadn't been reading his scriptures lately. Grijpstra hadn't either but he remembered Sunday school well enough. Grijpstra was disappointed at Mr. Bear's ignorance of the creation's order. He frantically waved his branch of peace.

Mr. Bear lumbered closer, drooling, growling, shaking long-nailed paws. His long snout gaped and showed big yellow teeth. He lolled a long pink wet tongue.

Grijpstra, feeling tired, sat down on a stump. This was like the storm at sea again, low tide sucking up currents, the void about to swallow his puny existence. Grijpstra remembered Ishmael's dream set in the airport restroom. He would like to argue with Saint Peter about things that unavoidably happen, unwilled by anything, whether divine or human. Grijpstra had been trying to do a good job, trying to make things happen just a little better for all parties concerned when mindless chance interfered again.

Very well. So there was only the meaningless moment.

Mr. Bear shuffled closer, on large soundless feet, stood up again, displayed matted fur covering his belly, raised his cheeks to bare chunky molars and wet canines, showed the whites of his eyes, which peered down on each side of a long drooling snout. The bear raised his arms, ready to come down on Grijpstra's shoulders.

On fear's far side all is friendliness again. "How are you doing, Mr. Bear?" Grijpstra asked.

The bear dropped its cheeks, snorted indifferently, turned, ambled off to the beach, splashed away, sank slowly until only his round furry head sat on the surface. The head, propelled by paddling feet below, floated off easily.

This was the moment to casually light the fat smelly type of cigar Nellie objected to, but Grijpstra wasn't carrying any.

Grijpstra entered the tunnel and saw a neat grave-sized hole.

The body had been covered with rocks, which now lay about. Maybe the bear intended to put them back after eating, to keep the competition away—foxes, raccoons maybe, coyotes, any of the predators Grijpstra had seen in the wildlife poster in Perkins' Sports Store window on Main Street.

Former Adjutant-Detective Grijpstra was somewhat used to corpses, and could diagnose their condition tentatively, while waiting for the pathologist's ultimate verdict. He mumbled through his handkerchief pressed against mouth and nose. "Female," Grijpstra whispered, shining his flashlight. "Caucasian," Grijpstra said. "Young adult. White-blond gossamer hair." He lifted a few strands with a twig. De Gier had said that. Lorraine with the gossamer

Scandinavian hair. Grijpstra checked the remains of a foot, determining it to be slender.

Mission accomplished. Correction. Almost accomplished. Step Two? Assist the murderer's escape.

Grijpstra ran about, thrashing through ferns and tall weeds. He yelled De Gier's name. De Gier showed up. De Gier was also yelling. "Hey!"

Grijpstra said no, he was not crazy. Come and look what he'd found.

They entered the tunnel. Grijpstra's flashlight shone brightly.

They exited the tunnel. De Gier staggered across the beach before vomiting between rocks covered with slimy seaweed.

"Yes," de Gier said.

"Lorraine?"

"Lorraine," de Gier said. He almost fell into Grijpstra's arms. "You know?"

"What?"

"You know," de Gier said, "I was sure I didn't do this. I thought it was something cooked up to hurt me." He turned, bent down again, splashed water on his face. "I was being clever. I thought I had reached an important point in my training, that I didn't have time to deal with people holding me back. So I got you to take care of it while I carried on regardless."

"Right," Grijpstra said kindly. "Prince Holy quests while Flatfoot slogs."

De Gier breathed deeply. "You think I'm an asshole."

"Oh yes," Grijpstra said kindly.

"There was more," de Gier said. "I missed you. I thought it would be nice to show you what I was doing here." He grimaced sadly. "As you said, Henk: showing off to Older Brother." De Gier pointed at the tunnel. "So I did kill her after all. I was too drunk to remember."

The incoming tide had almost floated the dinghy that Grijpstra had left on the beach. De Gier boarded it nimbly. Grijpstra wanted to get in too but the dinghy, forced into sudden speed by de Gier's powerful oar strokes, slipped from under Grijpstra's hands.

Grijpstra watched the dinghy get smaller as it left the channel between the islands, then reach the open ocean, an immense flat expanse, where it became a dot, then nothing.

Chapter 16

Grijpstra, wandering about Jeremy Island again, found an aluminum rowboat near Jeremy's former cabin. Rowing to the Point didn't take too long. He found a payphone at the Point's jetty. Grijpstra dialed.

"Sheriff's Office, Billy speaking. How may we help you?"

Billy Boy picked Grijpstra up in his jeep. He raised the *Kathy Three* by radio, specifying the dinghy's last-known location and direction.

"Not to worry," Billy Boy told Grijpstra. "They can't miss him on a clear night like this."

"He might take off again," said Grijpstra. "He's not in the best of moods, you know."

"Depressed?" Billy Boy seemed surprised. "Suicidal? Our nature lover? How come?"

Grijpstra explained that de Gier was not your average

balanced type. An alcoholic of de Gier's philosophical in-
clinations was likely to challenge fate at odd moments. He
and de Gier had been partying earlier that night, de Gier had
been drinking. The moon was full.

Billy Boy leaned over and sniffed Grijpstra's breath.
"Drinking alone, was he?"

Too true, Grijpstra affirmed. De Gier would do that,
get drunk on his own, go through sudden mood shifts,
become paranoid, wander off by himself.

The deputy sighed. "You wouldn't think so, Krip, but I
understand. Take de Gier now. Things may be going well
enough, here he is able to enjoy a summer in paradise,
something, could be any little thing, snaps—de Gier faces
the ravine."

Billy Boy touched Grijpstra's arm. "That's what I call it.
You kind of suddenly drop. You can drop through the
bottom. Maybe there's no bottom, Krip. Maybe there's a free
fall forever."

"Kind of frightening," Grijpstra said.

Billy Boy agreed. But there was another thing worth
discussing. "Take me now. You think I'm bad people, right?
Letting you go when *you* were in trouble." Billy Boy pointed
toward the sea. "About the same spot I would say, and I could let
your partner go now but this time I'll help out."

Bats flew around the parked jeep, excitedly squeaking
while diving at night moths. "Don't got much choice," Billy
Boy said. "As for me, I'd rather be making boat models but
here I am doing God knows what."

Grijpstra said he'd rather be painting dead ducks.

"Making models for a living," Billy Boy said. "Little lobster boats, every detail exact, I'd like that, Krip. But here I am, all preoccupied with being me and with my worries, letting you go at sea, storm and all." He laughed. "Wasn't that fun?"

Grijpstra didn't think it was fun.

"Listen," Billy Boy said. "Think of the other guy's fun for a change. Why be you?" He gestured. "Be me."

Grijpstra said that wasn't so easy.

"Let me illustrate." Billy Boy gestured. "All this land here was Indian land, you know that? Not so long ago. There were two tribes, one tribe to each shore. The bay was full of fish, not like now when the fishing industry scoops them up with sensitive machinery so there ain't none left. But back then, when we hadn't got around to doing away with fish yet, the Indians couldn't eat no fish either." He looked at Grijpstra. "Why not? Because the tribe this side of the bay kept spearing and shooting arrows at the other tribe from the other side of the bay. Anyone in a boat on a calm day sticks out and calm days are best for fishing. So the other tribe waits on the shore, aiming arrows from behind shrubs and long grasses and *Pyoo!*

"You got that?" Billy Boy asked.

Grijpstra, bouncing about as the jeep roared along the rough road, considered the situation. What if he said that he and de Gier didn't want to interfere with Hairy Harry's and Billy Boy's fishing. He tried to say that.

Billy Boy smiled.

"Can't we talk?" Grijpstra asked.

Not really, Billy Boy said. They could, of course, like the tribes had talked, endlessly, powwowing, humphing, promising never to bother each other but then there was the arrow again and the clear target: the temptation.

Billy Boy looked at Grijpstra, half-raised his eyebrows, half-dropped his eyelids: "Next time, Krip, when you see me, or I see you, all of us taking care of business, never mind who is in the boat, 'fishing,' as we call it"—Billy made quotation marks in the air—"never mind who is behind the bushes, arrow poised. *Pyoo!*"

"Doing away," Grijpstra said, "with your own fellow Indian. How would that make *you* feel?"

"It wouldn't," Billy Boy said.

Grijpstra got dropped off at Beth's Diner in Jameson. The *Kathy Three* came in and dropped off de Gier. De Gier rowed Grijpstra home to Squid Island. De Gier went to bed quietly, Grijpstra walked about quietly. On nearby Jeremy Island the empty cans shone in the moonlight.

Full moon always interfered with Grijpstrayan serenity, and there were the worries, of course. There was Lorraine, dead, there was taking care of business, there was de Gier's insanity, there were the empty cans on Jeremy Island, very visible.

Useless empties, spoiling a perfect view.

So there was something useful he could do now: clear up the mess. Grijpstra rowed across to pick up the useless empties.

Chapter 17

\There are good intentions, there is immense fatigue interfering with good intentions. Once Grijpstra had dragged the rowboat behind some boulders so that the sea wouldn't pick it up, he found a big boulder and sat on it. The tide receded steadily, leaving more beach, decorated with pebbles and clam shells. Grijpstra watched the slow undressing sleepily. He waved occasional mosquitos away while he ruminated on what could be expected, given the present scenario consisting of one dead Lorraine, one murdering de Gier, one unconnected Grijpstra. Intelligence, the commissaris claimed, is making optimal use of any given set of facts. How, Grijpstra thought, could he manipulate the given truths to serve his own survival? Rinus de Gier was a splendid fellow indeed—courageous, bizarre, musical, intelligent, curious, creative. Rinus de Gier was a goofy fellow indeed, suffering from a serious personality disorder. Not to be trusted. Hardly a partner to welcome into a private detective agency. De Gier was an expendable component of the given situation. Why not allow the sociopath to self-destruct? Then catch the bus, board El Al, kiss Nellie, settle down. Without friends, without worries.

Grijpstra, wobbly on his rock, dozed as Jeremy Island recreated itself in early morning light.

Squirrels set up a din in a pine tree.

They were the little Japanese alarm gadget that Nellie kept on the night table. Grijpstra reached to switch the squirrel alarm off. His morning, hardly started, had malfunctioned already. The automatic percolator hadn't brewed coffee. Nellie, most probably—Grijpstra hadn't opened his eyes yet—wasn't on her way to the bathroom either.

Grijpstra heard voices wishing the squirrels good morning. There was Aki's husky singsong voice and that of another woman, pleasant, gentle. There was also a metallic clatter that reminded him of another metallic clatter, his own and de Gier's, when they were putting down shiny beer cans.

Grijpstra jumped up, slipped on a wet rock, stubbed toes on roots, crashed through ferns and junipers. He slithered onto the beach. He saw two brightly colored fiberglass kayaks that had been pulled onto the ledge. He saw two pretty women bending over, who, straightening up, saw an older, portly man in a pinstriped three-piece suit crashing out of the island's foliage.

Aki dropped her bag of beer cans.

"Ha!" shouted Grijpstra at the other woman, the

woman in the Mother Earth T-shirt, the woman with the very short blond hair and the slender feet. "Ha!"

"This is Lorraine," Aki said. "This is Krip."

"Pleased to meet you," Lorraine said. "So you're Rinus's friend from Amsterdam, are you?"

"Ha!" shouted Grijpstra, hopping about on the foot that hurt less.

"How silly of us," Aki said. "All those nicely placed cans. I did think that this looked a bit like finding Easter eggs that the Easter Bunny had hidden. Are you the Easter Bunny, Krip?"

There was diminutive shouting from nearby Squid Island where de Gier, without his dinghy, ran about, wildly waving.

"How clever," Lorraine said, "and I thought you two were partying last night and would sleep in and give me a chance to clean up this awful mess here at daybreak."

"Got you," Grijpstra whispered. "Ha!"

Aki rowed the dinghy across to Squid Island to fetch de Gier.

"So what happened?" Grijpstra asked Lorraine, meanwhile, helping her to pick up more beer cans and wrappers. "I did see a small stain on the cliff."

"Well . . . ," Lorraine said.

"Wasn't pig blood or ketchup you brought along in a plastic bag with the specific premeditated purpose to set Rinus up?"

"No," Lorraine said.

"I'm sorry," Grijpstra said, "I have to ask. Ah . . . menstrual? Was it?"

"I'm not very regular," Lorraine said. "Haven't been lately. Hormonal imbalance. My age, maybe."

"Yes," Grijpstra said. "Yes. I'm sorry. I did notice that bloodstain. So . . . you were unwell?"

"I was," Lorraine said merrily. "I just wanted to stay the night. It started . . ."

"Ah . . . the bleeding . . . ?"

"Yes, as I kayaked to Squid Island," Lorraine said happily. "It gets bad sometimes. I may have lost a drop there."

"I'm sorry," Grijpstra said sadly.

"You got hangups about menstrual bleeding?" Lorraine asked. "Don't women bleed in Amsterdam?"

Grijpstra admitted the subject made him feel uncomfortable.

Lorraine laughed. "Right. De Gier was telling me. About sex, too. The blow-job case you guys solved when you were still cops in Amsterdam. You kept passing out."

Grijpstra wasn't familiar with the term "blow-job."

"Oral sex?" Lorraine pointed at her mouth, freshly made up to greet another day. "You know? Inserting the penis?"

Grijpstra staggered about the beach, dropping the cans he had just picked up.

"I don't believe this," Lorraine said. "You're like Beth's sister. She thought she had invented the technique and kept running to church to pray the new sin away. Isn't that amazing?"

Grijpstra looked at the safety of Squid Island where de Gier was getting into the dinghy that Aki had backed into his dock.

"You wanted to know about the bleeding," Lorraine said.

"Did Rinus push you?" Grijpstra asked.

"No," Lorraine said. "Not really. You see, he was drunk, or stoned, something terrible. Swaying, behaving idiotically, and I was standing on that stupid rock. . . ."

"A stone step," Grijpstra said.

"Yes, I took it for a stone step, but it was a rock, and Rinus leaned over to me, telling me to go home, over and over—men are repetitive while indulging—calling me *Nature Woman* with that silly British accent he puts on. It grates on the ears. Oh, he did get infuriating, and I wasn't feeling good."

"Night blind," Grijpstra said.

"What?"

"Rinus says you don't see too well in the dark."

"Yes," Lorraine said. "I couldn't go back, it was night by then, and then I fell and hurt myself and my period had started up much too early because of being so irregular, and I had no sanitary napkin, and then"—her voice became shrill—"Rinus just stepped back into the pagoda and put on that *record*."

"Miles Davis."

"Yes."

"Nefertiti."

"Yes."

"So Rinus didn't kick you when you were down," Grijpstra said.

"No."

"You weren't pregnant?"

"No," Lorraine said, "stupid Flash. That old boat needs repairs so Flash needs money and it all fit together. He saw an opportunity to get money to replace his boat, so he said I had been pregnant."

"But you weren't."

"No," Lorraine said. "I told them I was okay and to put me off at Bar Island and I was cursing de Gier . . ."

"Ah," Grijpstra said sadly.

". . . for being such an egotist. I always get furious when I have my period. During, not before; I'm different that way."

Grijpstra apologized.

"Grow up," Lorraine said. "Okay? So I hated the guy, and then Flash and Bad George came back later, to cut off my hair. They *said* they had this doll."

"Doll," Grijpstra said. "Did you see it?"

"I didn't see the doll," Lorraine said. "You ever been to the canning factory where Ishmael lives? Ishmael is a collector. He buys at yard sales. He keeps four stories of everything in that building. You think of something useless and Ishmael stocks it. Dolls too, I've seen them. Life-sized. Anything. Okay? So they were going to braid my hair into this doll's head and make Rinus believe it was me. Get him to pay for repairing their boat."

Grijpstra said, "But you never saw this doll."

"I'm not sorry," Lorraine said. "Men are just awful. Like your Rinus. He's worse."

"My Rinus," Grijpstra said.

"Came on heavy," Lorraine said. "I hate that."

Grijpstra looked at the blond head bending down.

"How's my hair?" Lorraine asked. "I shouldn't have let Bad George touch me with those big shears. Aki fixed it up a bit afterwards. Does it look bad?"

"Short hair," Grijpstra said, "becomes you."

"I guess I was hiding," Lorraine said. "I didn't want anyone to see me like this. You really think I look okay?"

De Gier arrived in the dinghy.

"Hi," Lorraine said.

"I'm sorry," de Gier said.

"He's really sorry," Aki said. "He's been saying he's sorry all the way from Squid Island to here. He's making it hard for you, Lorraine. He says he should have helped you out that evening. That he was egotistic again. That his advanced training should have shown him that You equals He."

"I'll never drink again," de Gier said.

"You're not an alcoholic," Lorraine said. "You're just an asshole."

"I think you two should kiss. And dance," Aki said.

Lorraine asked, "You think you would have been concerned, that fateful evening, if you had been sober?"

"I would have been concerned."

"And put me up?"

"Yes," de Gier said. "Alcohol made me do this to you. I am sorry."

Grijpstra had found his thermos. There was only one mug. Aki drank coffee first, then Lorraine, then de Gier. They cleaned up the beach together.

Aki and Lorraine, taking the garbage, paddled their kayaks to the Point, where Aki had left her car. Grijpstra took de Gier for a walk along Jeremy Island's shore. They sat down on a fallen trunk. De Gier patted his shirt pocket.

"You don't smoke anymore," Grijpstra said.

They watched the sea, rippled by the morning's breeze.

"So?"

"So," Grijpstra said, "we should get out of here."

"So who is the corpse?" de Gier asked.

Lorraine and her kayak were still in view. Sunlight reflected on Lorraine's short blond hair.

"Obviously, not Lorraine," Grijpstra said. "And if she wasn't Lorraine, then who cares?" He gestured. "An anonymous dead woman we have no knowledge of."

"How come the anonymous dead woman had Lorraine's hair?"

"Braided into her own hair," Grijpstra said. "By Bad George after he used a pair of rusty shears on Lorraine."

"El Al should have a flight out of Boston tonight," de Gier said. "We could be having dinner at Nellie's."

Grijpstra patted the side pocket of his jacket.

"You don't smoke anymore either," de Gier said.

"Are you happy now?" Grijpstra asked as he and de Gier moved across Jeremy Island. De Gier stopped dancing when Grijpstra said he wanted him to check out the remains of the anonymous woman's corpse in Mr. Bear's tunnel again.

"You recognize her?"

De Gier thought he did but it was hard to recognize a body that has been ravished by a bear.

"The *Macho Bandido* lady?" Grijpstra asked.

De Gier thought so, maybe.

"Had you met the *Macho Bandido* lady?"

De Gier had not but thought that the corpse matched the body Aki had described as belonging to the *Macho Bandido* lady.

"She who accompanied the three Latino sailors or alleged drug dealers who then disappeared in a rented limousine?"

De Gier thought so, maybe.

"Take a closer look."

De Gier tried to leave the tunnel. Grijpstra dragged him back and pushed him down.

De Gier was sure now.

"So you think it is likely that this corpse belonged to the beautiful lady who accompanied the three Latinos on the *Macho Bandido?*

"Yes." De Gier staggered out of the tunnel and ran toward the beach again.

"I think there is something here that might be figured out," Grijpstra said, squatting next to de Gier while de Gier washed his face with water scooped up from a puddle.

"I think you should phone Nellie," de Gier said, in between retching.

"Phone the commissaris?"

"We call that 'phoning Nellie' now," de Gier said, peering at Grijpstra with bloodshot eyes, "or connecting with Higher Judgment."

Chapter 18

"But of course," the commissaris said. "A party. That's what we need. Musical rallying of the troops. Good luck, Henk." He switched off his cordless telephone, gave it to his wife, and carefully maneuvered himself down the slippery garden steps.

She took the phone back into the house and returned to the garden. By then he was out of his chair and leaning on his stick, talking to the turtle, who, half-in, half-out of tall weeds, watched him attentively.

"I wish you'd lie down," Katrien said.

"Amazing, don't you think?" the commissaris asked Turtle. "All this rationalizing. You know what rationalizing means?"

Turtle, extending a scaly neck, didn't seem sure.

"Rationalizing means devising reasonable but untrue excuses to perform meaningful acts," the commissaris said.

"Turtle wants lettuce," Katrien said.

The commissaris had a few leaves in the pocket of his silk robe. He pulled one out. Turtle ate.

The commissaris turned to Katrien. "Grijpstra and de Gier pretend that they're these cool cucumbers, out there for kicks, but they're essentially do-gooders."

"Good for them," Katrien said.

"I've always been a do-gooder too." The commissaris prodded his own chest accusingly. "I find that amazing."

Katrien steered her husband back to his chair, gently pushed, made him sit down. "What's bad in doing good?"

"It's silly," the commissaris said. "So some unpleasant stuff is going on there involving third parties only. So what? My fine boys are guests in that great and beautiful country and de Gier inadvertently got himself into a little trouble and Grijpstra was good enough to get him out of it and that's it, Katrien." The commissaris nodded briefly. "Home, sweet home." He flicked his hand. "Home sweet home, Katrien. Our boy is off the hook. We all relax."

"But things aren't right there, Jan."

"Well," the commissaris said, "there may be mutual benefit in doing the good work, of course. If the investigation works out all parties involved might learn something." He held out more lettuce for Turtle. "Or feel better. This Aki maybe. And Beth."

"You don't care about Beth," Katrien said. "She isn't pretty. Remember that dinner party she threw for Grijpstra?

Grijpstra described Beth as a homely woman. You never care much for homely women."

The commissaris looked at Katrien. "I love homely women."

Katrien brought up another garden chair. "It's different with me. I'm old. You remember the way I looked before. There are photographs to remind you. And you need me more now." She frowned. "But maybe you are right. What has it got to do with us, what happened there? Grijpstra accomplished his mission and de Gier is probably still crazed. They'll be better off here."

"Tell them to try not to be heroes?"

"It's America," Katrien said. "Americans are so quick on the draw. That poor woman may have gotten herself cowboyed."

"Or Indianed," the commissaris agreed.

"An unnatural death brought about by that hairless sheriff just because he wanted the *Macho Bandido?*" Katrien asked.

The commissaris fed his last leaf of lettuce to Turtle. He softly scratched the reptile's head with the tip of his cane. He looked up. "Situations just happen along but when a good one runs into us"—he grinned—"why not try and use our good fortune?"

"This is a good situation?" Katrien asked. "With the bones of that poor woman being gnawed by Mr. Bear?"

The commissaris was staring at tall weeds growing

around his feet. "That kindly sheriff and Billy Boy, the frustrated model-boat builder—they are using the situation too. You know"—he patted her hand—"what else are bad guys doing but taking care of business . . . doing the best they can under the circumstances? Just the same as good guys. Imagine the situation out there, everybody growing pot on islands, a locally born and elected sheriff, what's he going to do? Arrest the town? Of course he joins his good old buddies, and being smarter he does better, and then greed takes over. Greed is a fat demon with a small mouth and whatever you feed it is never enough. I always have to laugh when I hear vindictive prosecutors sum up cases, pretending we have conscious criminals who willingly, by choice, create evil to hinder society. Bah . . . never happens that way. Never."

Katrien frowned. "Really, Jan. You call what the sheriff keeps doing unavoidable choice? How about clever self-serving manipulation of random circumstances?"

"Clever?" The commissaris reflected. "No. Unaware. Dragged down by circumstances. Poor Hairy Harry didn't pay attention. Started off okay, pleasing his mother in his new uniform, and then we see him slowly sliding down the chute of power, becoming a freak. Now what are we the well-intentioned to do? Given the world we live in, a power freak has to be done away with somehow." The commissaris patted Katrien's arm. "But let's do our moralizing later. For now we can theorize, fit our facts into some structure. Reconstruct reality." He smiled.

Katrien looked businesslike. "Reconstruct away."

"The sheriff," the commissaris said briskly, "boarded a million-dollar yacht, *Macho Bandido,* that was abandoned in Jameson Harbor." The commissaris held up a finger. "Situation one. You go from there, you're a lawyer too, Katrien."

Katrien touched Turtle's shield with her foot, rubbing it, making the animal stand firmly on its sturdy legs and close its eyes in pure enjoyment. "Situation two: We surmise that Hairy Harry found a woman aboard, the subject described by Aki as 'a model.' Subject was dead. There had been three men with her, South American types, with big drooping mustaches, golden bangles and chains, and tailormade sailor clothes. They were seen with the woman, partying on the yacht. This went on for some days. Then activity stopped, after Aki had seen a car, early one morning, probably a rented limo, pick up our yachtsmen at the dock. We assume the woman was left behind. Our witness, Aki, said it was still too dark to see who got into the limo. The luxurious vehicle arrived, people got in, the limo drove off. Hairy Harry knew that too. He or his deputy . . ."

"Billy Boy," the commissaris said. "The sheriff's office must keep an eye on the dock."

"Yes, Billy Boy saw it all." Katrien narrowed her eyes. "We keep presuming. The men leave, the woman doesn't, the yacht appears abandoned, he takes a peek aboard, finds the woman's dead body."

"Fits in, doesn't it?" The commissaris asked.

"The woman got overdosed?"

"Cocaine," the commissaris said. "We had a similar case right here in Amsterdam on the Emperor's Canal. Remember? Attractive young lady in a splendid gabled house in the best part of town gets herself coked up. She visits a few pubs and picks up three university students. She takes them home, parties, dies. We have an anonymous call, which de Gier, by following the victim's movements that evening, traced to one of the students who was with her when she died. Through him we located two more murder suspects. But, once again, we ran into a web of mishaps. Suspects stated that their hostess seemed insatiable, kept sniffing and handing out more cocaine, broke out the liquor, insisted on more sex. And she was enticing her partners—the cocaine kept exciting them too, of course, it does that in the early stages of the addiction . . .

". . . I thought it made the user paranoid?"

"Later, Katrien. Much later in the process. The user can't bear being touched then but first there's the sexy stage. As I said, subject kept inciting her guests and the students kept complying. She finally went into a dead faint that changed into a coma. One of the boys placed an anonymous call to a doctor, we verified that from the doctor's answering machine, and eventually called us."

"You believe the students were just trying to please?"

"Where does mutual pleasure become abuse?" the commissaris asked. "This model versus the Latinos could be a similar situation. Remember the boat show we visited during that holiday in Naples? Expensive yachts, beautiful saleswomen, champagne, smoked salmon on toast? You kept saying you thought some of the buyers had to be big-time dope dealers. Same here. South American types pick up a brand new beautifully equipped yacht, the saleswoman, 'the model,' goes along on the maiden voyage." He stared at Katrien. "Can you see it? The cocktail party on board? The clients joking that they'll buy the boat for cash if the seller throws in the girl too? Everybody hopped up on something or other. Everything seems just beautiful and easy. The seller takes the model aside and offers her a commission in cash if she goes along with the joke. The buyers are happy with their new boat, the model is happy with the prospect of profit-sharing, a week of partying and beautiful island hopping—quite risky, of course, as in our present case where the joy ride becomes a hair-raising trip up the dangerous Maine coast. The Latinos do manage to make it to Jameson, the effort warrants a party, pot plus whiskey and a wild wild woman, things get out of hand—we have a dead woman. . . ."

"But the South American types didn't call a doctor and the police anonymously," Katrien said, "like our nice university student on the Emperor's canal."

"All situations differ because happenstance cannot repeat itself exactly," the commissaris said. "We may safely assume that foreign suspects will not want a tough American sheriff to check out their boat. As soon as their beautiful lady becomes seriously unwell, suspects decide to run for freedom. Abandoning a million dollars' worth of yacht means nothing to them and it might stall the sheriff, like throwing a bone to the wolf that pursues you."

"Why didn't suspects attempt to hide the body? Throw her overboard themselves? Bury her on an island somewhere?" Katrien shook her head. "But they didn't. The yacht was left in Jameson Harbor, anchored with a short line that made her dip her nose at low tide."

"Too hung over from that final party?" the commissaris asked. "It would mean taking the boat out of Jameson Harbor, facing shoals and tides and currents and winds once more. I bet you they swore they'd never handle that boat again."

"So now the sheriff arranges for *Macho Bandido* to break her anchor rope so that she may float into the ocean where he can claim it privately. But the dead woman is in his way so *he* gets rid of the corpse?"

"Chucks it overboard," the commissaris said.

"Or buries it on Jeremy Island," Katrien said. "Either possibility works. Flash and Bad George either saw Hairy Harry carry something ashore at the island or they found the body floating in the bay, maybe as they were taking Lorraine home. But in that case Lorraine would know about there being a dead body." Katrien shook her head. "Too gory, she wouldn't have cooperated. So, Flash and Bad George picked up the corpse *before* they met with Lorraine, and buried it in the tunnel. Noticing a similarity between the 'model's and Lorraine's bodies, they later dug it up to frighten de Gier and thought of a ruse to get Lorraine to cut off her hair. They then braided that into the corpse's . . ."

"What about the sheriff and Billy Boy knowing about the tunnel on Jeremy Island?" the commissaris asked. "They were kids once, grew up around Jameson. Kids love tunnels, so do hibernating bears. Having something to hide, they thought of their tunnel. Flash and Bad George also knew about the tunnel. So did Mr. Bear. The two skippers watched the sheriff doing something sneaky on Jeremy Island, traced him, Mr. Bear traced them. They were all in there, burying the poor woman, digging her up again."

Katrien looked sad. "Kids. And now our kids are out there. Playing. Without you to protect them. They aren't even armed."

"I think de Gier would like to show us that he can lace his own boots now," the commissaris said. "And Grijpstra was getting stuck here, all on his own. I'm sure he enjoys working with his old pal again."

While Katrien went shopping, the commissaris explained to Turtle that Grijpstra and de Gier, realizing their weak position, were applying for help from available sources. Who were? Beautiful Aki, powerful Beth, Mother Farnsworth in her doggie shape, handyman/collector Ishmael, disciple of Hermit Jeremy, the two skippers. The commissaris was swishing his cane through the quiet garden air, cutting down Hairy Harry. "My two lean warriors, Turtle, temporarily slowed down by bags of money; a mere detail we'll fix later." Being at it anyway, the commissaris also swished Billy Boy.

Dinnertime came along. "The way I see it," the commissaris said brightly, "there's been some regrouping, some crossing over lines. Our boys have made friends there."

"Two retards in a sinking boat?" Katrien asked. "A dog with braids? A madman flying a motorized kite with a fuel-pump problem? An obese short-order cook and her disoriented recovering lady love? The past-her-prime biologist?"

"Others who can be helpful habitually come the way they are," the commissaris said, "not the way you may want them to present themselves." The commissaris shook his fist. "To the barricades, comrades!"

"We're opposed by bizarre evil, Jan."

The commissaris said, "I believe the United States to be basically sound, and moreover the best possible country ever. In spite of what goes on. Americans do keep trying. And all my heroes come from there, Katrien. Were there ever finer idealists than Washington, Jefferson, and Franklin? If you think of a superior man, doesn't Abraham Lincoln come to mind? Could anyone be more sensitive and creative than Clifford Brown and Miles Davis? The subtle juggling of W. C. Fields, Katrien, the ultimate in managing telephone books and words. Even the American shadowside is brilliant. Dennis Hopper, for instance, and Harry . . ."

"Dirty Harry?" Katrien asked.

The commissaris frowned. "No, no. Harry . . . ," he

smiled. "Harry Dean Stanton, my dear. A most wonderful actor."

Katrien felt guided by Eleanor Roosevelt, Aretha Franklin, and Flannery O'Connor.

Later, in bed, Katrien said maybe it had to happen—silly de Gier, with his going-nowhere affairs, ultimately humiliated by Nature Woman.

"I think you should call the boys back now, Jan."

The commissaris, about to fall asleep, reopened an eye. "What?"

"They'll lose out," Katrien said. "Call them back. You aren't there and Hairy Harry and Billy Boy have that awful little man guiding them, that Bildah . . ." She turned her head toward him. "I think he looks like you."

"If so he can't be all bad," the commissaris said.

They lay quietly, feet touching, until the commissaris's leg jerked and he was mumbling in his sleep.

"Jan! I can't sleep when you mumble."

His foot nudged hers. "We could do it ourselves."

Chapter 19

The party came about naturally, after the sinking of *Kathy Three,* a few days later. Flash Farnsworth claimed Hairy Harry had used a bazooka borrowed from friends in the National Guard. Bad George thought the sheriff might just as easily have tapped the boat with a hammer.

The company was eating lobsters at Beth's Diner—Grijpstra's treat—properly, in the Maine tourist manner, with plastic bibs tied around their necks by Aki. Each bib showed a jolly lobster, waving happily, elated by the prospect of being boiled alive.

"Lobbah Lobstah, by Walt Disnah," Bad George said, drinking beer. He wanted Grijpstra and de Gier to drink too, for this was a farewell party of despair, as he didn't know what he and Flash would do without their vessel. He himself had not tasted alcohol since his car was hit by a drunk and his wife had died and he himself got this face that would look the same forever "aftah."

"Why bothah?" Bad George asked.

Flash Farnsworth—between tearing his lobster apart and going through the motions of tipping his bottle to keep Bad George company—presented his Bunny dream to amuse hosts and guests. "The Walt Disnah Bunnah." The Disney Bunny hopped through Flash's dream, being ever so cute wearing a red ribbon, singing away, until Kathy Two picked it up quietly and shook the bunny until it was dead.

"Don't need no more bullshit bunny," Flash said.

"No bullshit about Mr. Bear," Grijpstra said. "I met Mr. Bear on Jeremy Island, eating a lady."

Bad George wasn't listening. He told the tale "Bears at the Dump," which had to do with a younger, less bad George, whose then-still-living wife bought him a camera for his birthday. Next day George was going to get himself some bears on film. The bears, at daybreak, were sorting garbage, and Bad George was focusing his Kodak, not noticing that the bears were between Bad George and Bad George's vehicle, and were closing in.

Flash Farnsworth had heard Grijpstra.

"So what did you do, Krip, when you saw Mr. Bear eating the lady on Jeremy Island??"

"I sat down," Grijpstra said.

"What else did you do?"

"I gave up on everything."

"Got to be respectful," Bad George said, listening now.

"Always talk nicely to Mr. Bear. From the heart. Like me, at the dump." He pounded his own heart. "Krip?"

Grijpstra looked up, lobster claw in hand. "Yes, Bad George?"

"Krip, you weren't trying to take that dead lady away from Mr. Bear, were you?"

Grijpstra cracked the claw, pulled out white meat, dipped it in butter, filled up most of his mouth, chewed, swallowed, looked pleased. "Aaaaah."

"Were you, Krip? To see what she looked like? Her hair and feet and all?"

A silence kept stretching. Everybody ate lobster, cracking, sucking, digging, dipping, chewing.

Grijpstra looked at de Gier. He half-dropped an eyelid.

"A bazooka?" de Gier asked on cue. "*Kathy Three* really was hit by a bazooka?"

Bad George looked at Flash. His head bent forward briefly.

"Hairy Harry don't like us much," Flash Farnsworth said, "on account of what we know, taking *Kathy Three* out all the time, seeing things at sea. He don't know we don't tell nuthin'. No use telling when nobody don't do nuthin' nohow." Flash nodded solemnly. "But the sheriff keeps seeing us watching those salt bags hitting the sea near Rogue Island and he worries. So he sinks our tub." Flash shrugged. "No boat, can't see nuthin', don't tell nuthin'."

"Scarin' us like that," Bad George said. "Sinking the *Kathy Three*."

Aki brought more sour-dough biscuits to go with the lobsters. Kathy Two pushed a wet nose into Grijpstra's hand. Grijpstra dropped a biscuit on the floor. The dog pushed it around for a bit. "Got to sop it in butter first," Aki said, giving it back to Grijpstra. Grijpstra dunked the biscuit, apologized to Kathy Two, handed it down again. Kathy Two wagged her tail once, accepted the biscuit by gently holding on to it, front teeth only, before backing away, sitting down, dropping the treat, sniffing it in a careful and appreciative manner, picking it up again. She ate delicately.

Grijpstra commented on the dog's dignity.

"Been working on her some." Flash looked fierce. "She's learned a bit this time around, hasn't she?"

"You don't beat her, do you?" de Gier asked.

Flash hid his hands in his beard. "Can't expect a man to beat his mother nohow."

"So," de Gier said, in between sucking meat out of a spindly lobster leg, "Hairy Harry or Billy Boy put a missile through the *Kathy Three?*"

"Them fellers will do anything," Flash said. "Them fellers got the weapons."

"Who knows what they did exactly?"

Bad George explained that he and Flash had left the boat on a mooring in Jameson Harbor with the tide going out. He himself caught the bus to visit family, and Flash was doing town things, getting supplies, stopping off everywhere, socializing, "fixin' up the world." But you can't fix the world, Bad George explained. You could, maybe, try to survive a while. "Like them dinosaurs when they heard the meteor was comin'."

"Ain't easy survivin' without the *Kathy Three*," Flash Farnsworth said.

Grijpstra, wanting to hear Aki's song again—the waitress's chant, as de Gier called it: "*Buddah . . . Mikkelah . . . Heineka*"—ordered more beer. He asked Bad George to elaborate on the loss of the *Kathy Three*.

"Like with the *Macho Bandido*," Bad George said.

De Gier knew about that. Released from his guilt now that Lorraine sat next to him, her thigh touching his, de Gier reported on work done in his new capacity, that of assistant to Private Investigator Grijpstra. De Gier had rowed out to where the yacht was anchored, fished up the anchor with a dragline, ascertained that the anchor cable had been cut. "Snipped, probably with wire cutters. That cable never broke from natural causes."

"Sheriff saw you fishin' for that cable?" Flash asked.

"Billy Boy was driving by," de Gier said.

"Might be getting in the bazooka's sights yerself," Flash said.

"Sheriff just used a regular hammer," Bad George replied to Grijpstra's query. "*Kathy Three* was so rotten, all she needed was a tap on a waterline board. The cracked board would sink her once the current sucked her out of the harbor."

There was a moment of silence, a wake, to thank the old cabin cruiser for having been around so long, so usefully, and pleasurably. The company sent sympathy toward DeLorean Ledge, where *Kathy Three* was a wreck now, being slowly crushed by easy flowing waves, three miles out of Jameson, where Ishmael had located the dying vessel, looking down from his plane, radioing the message into Beth's Diner, adding that he would be joining the party shortly.

"What to do?" Flash asked.

"Buy a new boat," Grijpstra said. "What else?"

How could Mr. Moneybags Eurodollar, asked Bad George, sit there and make such an exaggerated statement? A new boat the size of the former *Kathy Three*, a pleasure cruiser built as sturdily as a work boat, a new boat made out of new-fangled fiberglass (for no one used wood now, there wasn't any left), a new comparable vessel would cost over a hundred thousand dollars.

"Here's what you do, Bad George," Grijpstra said. "You get yourself one hundred thousand dollars, say a hundred and twenty thousand dollars' worth of new vessel, complete with radar and loran and radio and depth finders and whatnot, rafts and dories, cabin heater, a refrigerator full of Buddah . . . Mikkelah . . . Heineka," Grijpstra sang, "a water heater for the shower. . . ."

"Flash Farnsworth don't shower much," Bad George said.

"Don't you agree, Bad George?" de Gier asked reasonably. "Isn't poverty just a state of mind, an attitude, if you will?"

Bad George, exhilarated by another beer, agreed that

he and Flash would welcome an elevated state of mind producing the right attitude providing creative thinking that would have him and Flash boating about in *Kathy Four*. But just say, for argument's sake, that a fairy godmother granted the wish you were thinking of—this is America, if you don't have it, you import it. . . .

Flash wanted to know if Catherine Deneuve could come along.

De Gier smiled. "That's better."

They were all cruising nicely at fifteen knots an hour, at five gallons of fuel an hour, to Eggemoggin Reach, Merchant's Row, and other magic thoroughfares south of the Twilight Zone, remote waterways the *Kathy Three* could never quite get to, when Flash pointed out that they hadn't done away with the sheriff's bazooka.

"POW!" shouted Flash.

Ishmael came in. Aki pulled up a chair. "How're you doin', Ishmael?"

Ishmael was doing just fine. He'd been flying up till a few hours ago. Until his plane got shot down. He'd almost got shot down himself. Ishmael held up a leg to show a graze mark on his boot.

"Bullet," Flash said.

"Terminated the Tailorcraft," Ishmael said. He smiled bravely. It had been an adventure. Of course, he never thought he could land a disabled airplane against a hillside, at a forty-five-degree angle. Who had done the shooting? Ishmael wasn't too sure but later, after he scrambled down the hill's slope and reached the highway, there was friendly Hairy Harry offering a lift, and there was a scoped rifle in the Bronco, the nine-millimeter Mauser the sheriff was so fond of. Hairy Harry had been target practicing that afternoon. He told Ishmael he particularly liked hitting flying targets.

"Warning shots," said Beth, who had cooked up another lobster for Ishmael, even though the kitchen was closed.

Lorraine thought so too.

"Warning who?" Grijpstra asked.

"Warning you?" Aki asked.

Ishmael wondered what to do without an airplane.

"You get a new plane," Flash Farnsworth said. "Poverty is a state of mind."

Ishmael agreed that a spic-and-span, spanking-new Cessna, feather light, fast even at impulse speed, was what was needed here. But say, for argument's sake, that he actualized himself an aircraft, wouldn't he still be a flying target?

"POW!" shouted Bad George.

They were still laughing when Billy Boy stopped his jeep in the twilight outside the diner, raised his wrist, studied his watch.

"Can't serve beer after closing time," said Beth.

"My place?" Ishmael asked.

Loaded in de Gier's Ford product and Beth's bus, the party drove to Ishmael's old canning factory at the Point. Kathy Two sat on Grijpstra's lap, sticking out her braid-ears, looking out the Ford's side window, her twenty muscular toes massaging Grijpstra's thighs pleasurably. Grijpstra wondered how he could get Nellie and de Gier's cat Tabriz to agree to have a Kathy Two look-alike share their castle.

"Just ask them," de Gier said.

Grijpstra never liked it when de Gier was telepathic.

Chapter 20

The abandoned canning factory, de Gier had been told by Flash Farnsworth, contained the complete collection of What.

"Of what?"

Little Flash, weighed down by his bird-nest hairdo, deranged leprechaun in green coveralls and boots, rolling about on a damaged pelvis, might have embellished. "But he's close enough," Grijpstra said, following Ishmael, in charge of the tour. The cannery was square. It hid behind tall brick-faced cracked walls, and peered at the visitors out of half-shuttered windows, like half-glasses on an old man's face. The big building was overgrown with ivy, turning red at autumn's approach. There was a yard surrounded by sheds. The sheds contained cars, same make: Ford, same model: Pinto.

"Nobody wants Pintos," Bad George said. "He got them all for free."

"Because their gas tanks were supposed to blow up," Flash said. "Not that they did."

Ishmael explained his "theory of contrariwise": Collect out of fashion, be rich on no money.

"Why collect thirty-two identical giveaway motorcars?" Ishmael asked rhetorically. Ishmael explained his "theory of magic multiplication": Placement of identical objects achieves a magical effect. In multiplication possibilities increase magically. Ishmael pointed out the splendor in the placing of identical Pintos facing each other, in four Pintos diagonally arranged, in Pintos mounting another, in upside-down Pintos underneath themselves, in Pintos resting on their sides, tires touching.

"Like making love to twins?" de Gier asked Lorraine.

Beth thought the idea exciting. She suggested going to Hawaii to find identical Akis.

"Identical Beths too?" Aki asked.

There were other demonstrations of multiple magic. Ishmael showed them three objects, overgrown with dried seaweed and lichens. The objects were identical, nonidentifiable, and had been brought up by divers salvaging a sunken freighter in Jameson Bay. There was a light bulb illuminating the arrangement displayed on a trestle table.

"Untitled," Ishmael said proudly.

There were also collections of the similar nonidentical: rusted bird cages hung in the yard, some with toy birds inside, all with open doors. "Predicament in Birdland," Ishmael said. "Free to go, but where to? Like the crazy man in the Eastern Maine Mental Hospital. Kept in a cage near the nurses' station. He's being good so they open the cage, but he won't step out. He does step out when prodded, but he sits outside, one hand clutching a bar behind him. That's the way he feels safe.

"That was you?" Grijpstra asked.

No other, Ishmael explained. He had given up on religion at the time, had been institutionalized (due to odd behavior), while trying to deal with nothing. But he wasn't ready yet: no free fall for Ishmael while still holding on to his cage.

"It ain't easy," Beth said. "Makes some people fat."

Once inside the cannery there was a doll collection, arrays of tools, masks, neatly labeled boxes on shelves containing nails, screws, washers, nuts, handles, and hinges, writing implements, brushes, pens, fittings, light bulbs and tubes, cutlery, assorted hardware. Ishmael liked sorting through cast-offs, leftovers after yard sales that he would pick up in a Pinto. Not that he intended to save waste. The entire universe might be waste. The universe could save itself.

"You give this away?" de Gier asked. "Suppose somebody needs something?"

"Come and get it," Ishmael said. "Step right up."

"Art," Grijpstra said, admiring more Pintos. "*This* is Art."

Not really, Ishmael said. Just something to do inside on rainy days. Or outside, weather permitting.

Kathy Two, woofing, asked Grijpstra to carry her up a

flight of narrow steps, too steep for her to manage. The cannery's second floor displayed bookend owls, of stone and other materials, ugly and moody looking, and models of flying dinosaurs suspended from ceilings—some were skeletons that glowed in the dark, some had leathery wings.

"Uselessly wise," Ishmael said. "Beautifully extinct."

There was also an obstacle course that Kathy Two used for performing tricks: leaping through hoops, sitting on a swing pushed by Ishmael, jumping across bars, finishing up by sitting patiently on a stool, both paws up, looking expectant. "Good Kathy Two," everyone said. There was applause. The dog smiled shyly.

"She's learnin'," Flash said.

"Kathy One was rude," Bad George said, "never even gave you the time of the day."

"Not so easy," Ishmael said. "Living on food stamps in a burned-out trailer, keeping a drunk bum of a husband, having Flash for a son."

"She had excuses," Flash agreed, "but never good enough. I told her she'd have to come back as a dog. There she is." He kissed the dog.

Kathy Two snarled.

"I'll be a dog next time I have to come back," Beth told Aki. "You can say you've been there but you don't live long and you sleep most of it."

The music room was part of the third floor, with arrangements from the thirties. Ishmael pulled out picture books to show Art Deco sources. The music room's wain-

.coting was dappled maple out of a lumberyard fire sale. The higher part of the walls was lizard leather, peeled off a shipment of waterlogged ladies' shoes. Tulip-shaped lamp shades were glued together from colored stained-glass shards.

"You just run into this?" Grijpstra asked.

"It just runs into me," Ishmael said.

"What if you lost the collection?" Grijpstra asked.

Ishmael thought that might be nice too.

Musical instruments were everywhere, centered by a set of drums that Grijpstra arranged around himself, a valve trombone that Beth could play, a saxello, three sets of tablas, a doussn' gouni, and a lyricon that Bad George tried but couldn't do all that much with, a dented and dirty trumpet that de Gier picked up, pods of various sizes, a gourd guitar that Flash put down because of broken strings, Ishmael's own upright piano. They couldn't play yet because Flash and Bad George still wandered about, trying things out. A melodica? No. An acoustic bass? Bad George claimed the bass. He found Flash a tuba.

"Good," Grijpstra said, stirring soup with brushes on the snare drum, sideswiping a ride cymbal, setting up an up-tempo groove for everyone else. He worked the crash-cymbal too. "'Bemsha Swing'?" The bass drum thumped. De Gier blew the trumpet. "Beh."

The *beh* didn't go anywhere, not even when Bad George matched it on bass. Grijpstra never left the groove, singing Thelonious's tune to help things along. Bad George caught on, walked the changes, supported the groove. Ishmael came in too. He had heard "Bemsha Swing" on de Gier's sound equipment, had tried it before, repeated the theme now, in high note clusters on the upright piano. Flash's tuba put in a hoot that hit it right, encouraging Beth to come in on trombone. Aki sang. Lorraine rang some cowbells.

The ensemble was off then, without de Gier. De Gier shook debris out of his trumpet—a previous player's solid saliva (it was a wonder he didn't get sick), a rat's nest—risking bubonic plague just for a little music; what he wouldn't do for others, he said later.

Waiting for de Gier to front on his horn, the ensemble produced waves of rhythm, held steady by Grijpstra on brushed cymbals and snare drum. Trombone and voice harmonized, structured by Bad George on the bass. Flash, barely breathing into the tuba, helped shape the duet. Ishmael trilled more piano notes.

De Gier kept trying. "Beh."

"Tuh *TAH!*" the trumpet sang finally. They all had it then. Lorraine too, shaking the theme on a tambourine.

After "Bemsha Swing" came "Endless Blues," de Gier's own composition. The trumpet cried some. Aki's voice cried too. Grijpstra rolled his toms ecstatically, for he was back in the dory, facing Nellie, and Hokusai waves. He played the waves on cymbals. Bad George sounded Mr. Bear's slow footsteps on the bass. Aki sang the loon's chuckle. Coyotes wailed again on the trumpet but there were also the lava beaches of Hawaii's Kona Coast, mostly in duets of trombone and voice, with long subdued notes to indicate sunsets, volcanos glowing at night, sun-shot froth on cresting waves. Little intricacies on piano and dry ticking against the side of Grijpstra's snare drum supplied contrasts between scenes, also discipline to contain melodrama. A solo by Bad George on the bass, which he brushed gently with an almost hairless bow, impressed Kathy Two so much that she rolled over to display a pink belly, before jumping up to bark sharply. There were car engines growling outside, cutting out when Billy Boy's voice shouted commands. Then there was Hairy Harry's posse stamping up the cannery's stairs.

Chapter 21

Being instructed not to shun force while exercising a warrant to search the cannery for illegal warehousing of controlled substances, the posse smashed most of Ishmael's collection of What. There was also some prodding with nightsticks and name-calling in gruff voices. "Tongue and Groovers" referred to Beth and Aki, "Short Retards" covered the skippers, "Aliens in the Mist," "Hippy-Yippy," and "New-Born Nihilist" took care of the others.

Most of Ishmael's arrangements were no longer intact after half a dozen deputies, flown in from remote corners of the Twilight Zone, in storm-trooper boots and Boy Scout hats, ran out of breath.

Nothing much found, nothing much left.

The posse departed as it had come. All-terrain vehicles roared and drove off with squealing tires.

There were no wounded, only bruised: Beth on the buttock, Bad George on the shoulder.

"Oh dear, oh dear," Grijpstra sympathized, surveying what was left of a flying dinosaur's twenty-foot leathery wingspan, kicking broken owls aside, keeping Kathy Two away from smashed jars.

De Gier held up a bear mask, found under rubble the marauding deputies had thrown out of windows. He checked the mask's labels. One said REFUSE IMPORTS; the other, MADE IN CHINA.

Aki put it on. "Can I have this, Ishmael?"

"Sure," Ishmael said. He mentioned his "joyful destruction theory." "Dinosaurs had it good for millions of years. Then the thing got old and they were happy to leave." He spread his arms. "We can't have too much destruction."

Beth agreed. The collection of What had indeed gotten old. She had noticed cobwebs.

"Haven't been looking at this stuff much lately," Ishmael said, shoving remnants aside. Ishmael's living quarters and guest rooms, carefully arranged showcases of furniture from the forties and the fifties, complete with period books, drapes, carpets, and appliances, had been smashed and ripped by the diligent deputies, then kicked into corners.

De Gier invited all homeless persons to sleep in the pagoda.

Lorraine paddled home to Bar Island holding de Gier's pen-size but ultra-strong flashlight in her teeth. She didn't really want to as—Beth pointed out—there might be associations, but she didn't want to leave her kayak either and she was night-blind. Beth and Aki drove back to Jameson. Grijpstra and Ishmael rowed dinghies from the Point to Squid Island. Ishmael took de Gier and Bad George, talking about the challenge of space. For once he'd clean up the cannery and have a bonfire in the yard. He'd have four stories of space, to fill at will. Ishmael felt excited. He developed his theory of pre-creation, which had to do with serenity, from which creation would start herself up again.

"We're friends now?" Grijpstra asked Flash in the other rowboat. "Remember Mr. Bear eating the dead lady in the tunnel? Care to tell me who dug the dead lady's grave?"

"Never dug no grave in no tunnel," Flash Farnsworth said. He admitted to seeing Hairy Harry and Billy Boy carrying in the corpse. But the idea of digging her up to fool de Gier was Flash's. "What with your pal drunk as a skunk, didn't know what or nuthin' . . ."

"Never knows what or nuthin'", Grijpstra said.

"Didn't work out too good," Flash said. "Worse now, right, Krip? No boat. No airplane. Cannery all stoved in. Hairy Harry gettin' stronger. Damn tootin' right I'm a rebel. We'll make it work again. Remember Pearl Harbor, Krip? But now I'm tired."

"Europe to the rescue," Grijpstra said, pulling the oars. One oar slipped, he fell over backward.

Flash tittered.

De Gier was waiting on Squid Island's dock. "You bed them all down for the night," Grijpstra said, "and give me the key to the Ford product, please."

"Phone the netherworld," de Gier asked. "Cross the final frontier. Call on the ogres. Release revenge."

Chapter 22

"Maybe we should do this," the commissaris said, tapping the table where he had spread his maps.

Katrien wasn't sure.

The commissaris rested his finger on Rogue Island. "But, Katrien . . ."

"But they're dealing with the sheriff of Woodcock County," Katrien said, "with an elected official. Please, Jan, this is a civilized world now, there must be better ways. Tell them to have the villain arrested. . . ."

"How?"

"The DEA," Katrien said.

"Ineffective," the commissaris said. "Remember that marijuana shipment?" His finger prodded the map. "Right here, on Bar Island. Aki had that all planned out for them, there were agents behind every bush. The bad guys still won."

"America is a democracy, Jan."

"So is Holland," the commissaris said, "and little Jimmy next door got AIDS while prostituting himself to get cash to buy crack."

"You said there were no bad guys," Katrien said. "That things just happen."

"Let's happen along too." The commissaris rubbed his hands together. "Let's be sly, Katrien."

Katrien made a face.

"If only you could be a little bit more negative," the commissaris said gleefully. "You know what we have here, Katrien? Tribal warfare." He pointed. "Check that encyclopedia. Read up on Native American East Coast tribes. You'll find that the Iroquois were fierce and the Algonquins were sly. They had fun together."

"Scalping," Katrien said. "Torture. We're beyond that now."

"We're never beyond violence," the commissaris said. "This kind could be fun. Know your enemy, Katrien. Hairy Harry is a paranoid Iroquois. He firmly believes Grijpstra and de Gier will interfere with his drug operation, and all this stealing of yachts, hiding of corpses, shooting of airplanes, willful destruction of a little dog's obstacle course is his brand of defense. Fear makes him twist facts. He never knew about Lorraine's disappearance, never cared either. He sees Grijpstra the Algonquin telephone overseas, reporting to someone. To the Big Guy Back Home."

Katrien kissed his cheek. "Chief Jan of the Algonquin."

"De Gier was in Maine before," the commissaris said. "The state police flew him into Jameson. Maybe a legend started up then. Ishmael knew Jeremy. Jeremy the hermit knew me. I was chief of detectives."

The commissaris found his cane, limped to the porch, descended to the garden.

Katrien, by watching his lips, caught most of what the commissaris said to Turtle.

"Tribal warfare," the commissaris told Turtle. "Katrien is still an idealist. I'm not saying she isn't right, but we act on lower levels here, within desire and fear. Fierce warriors threaten us peaceful people.

"Rationalizing our interference, Turtle? Certainly. We need an excuse. The war on drugs? Well, maybe yes, although I'm all for pot myself. The weed of procrastination slowing down pollution. How about *Sheriff Shoots Eagle?*

"Okay? Okay.

"Turtle?

"No ordinary violence, Chieftain Katrien advises? Make use of the magic way, you say? Do I remember the shaman under the banyan tree, Milne Bay, New Guinea?

"Sure, sure, Turtle, we didn't send de Gier to the end of the world for nothing, did we now?

"Yes, Turtle, I do remember de Gier's report on the method of Pointing the Bone, oh yes, I do.

"How that works? Piece of cake. Get a bone. Get some powerful minds to help. Point the bone at the paranoid Iroquois. Visualize effects. That sheriff dies.

"Yes?

"Have a tribal powwow first? Get a tribal mandate?

"Yes. Must follow proper protocol, Turtle. You're a good counselor. I thank you kindly."

"Oh dear," Katrien said, watching the commissaris climb the garden steps.

"Katrien?"

"Now what, Jan?"

"I wonder," the commissaris said. "That leg of lamb I saw in the freezer? How about cooking that up sometime, say tomorrow?"

"With Brussels endive, Jan?"

"Delicious," the commissaris said. "Isn't Nellie very fond of Belgian endive? Why don't I ask her over? And while I'm at it, I'll put a call in to Beth's Diner too. Get things going again, my dear."

He limped to the phone, leaning on his cane, swinging his free arm martially.

Chapter 23

"Look what I made in therapy, folks," Lorraine said.

Lorraine had kayaked over from Bar Island and brought her war pipe, an artifact she had made herself, copied from a museum piece on view in Jameson's town hall.

Lorraine believed in using local materials to evoke local power. The pipe's stem was "moose wood," a type of willow, hollowed out with a stone awl dating back to a Penobscot village that preceded Jameson. She had found it on the beach. The pipe's bowl was birch she had cut herself. The raccoon-skin thong wrapped round the stem was part of a worn-out Seminole sandal, bought at an Indian road stall in the Florida Everglades. Five long feathers shed by Jameson Bay eagles, later dyed blood red with the juice of cranberries, had been found on the shore by Lorraine and Aki.

Bad George set the kitchen table in the pagoda. Flash

baked biscuits and passed them out. Ishmael created a study in apple slices and grapefruit. Bad George had fried bacon dripping on paper napkins and an omelette puffing up on the stove.

They ate first, while the war pipe, a sinister presence in spite of their tribal banter, dangled from fishing thread attached to the kitchen lamp by de Gier.

Lorraine had brought tobacco too, Drum, in a plastic bag.

"Made in Holland," de Gier said, reading the plastic bag's print.

There was no shortage of omens.

"Beth?" Ishmael said into the CB radio's microphone. "Would you and Aki join us for coffee? I'll be picking you up at the dock at the Point."

Beth, being boss, got to untie the war pipe from the kitchen lamp. Lorraine stuffed the pipe's bowl with Drum shag tobacco. Aki lit the match.

The warriors puffed on the war pipe in turns.

"We condemn the accused?" Beth asked when the pipe passed back to her.

Bad George raised his hand. "For trying to kill Krip here by not picking him up when he was sucked east by the ocean in Little Max's dory."

"Humph," said the congregation.

"For sinking the *Kathy Three* by cutting her free and tapping her rotten bottom with a hammer."

"Humph."

"For willful destruction of Ishmael's Tailorcraft and of his collection of What."

"Humph."

"But that's okay," Ishmael said. "I'm going to do this new depth thing in the cannery now, with the colors. I still have those cans of yellow and orange paint and those sheets of old plywood. What I'm trying to achieve is some experiments with depth. You see . . ."

The group applied peer pressure by staring.

"I'll just humph on the Tailorcraft," Ishmael said. "Okay?"

"Killing loons?" Flash asked. "Mallards? That dolphin? Bears?"

"Humph."

Beth raised her hand. "For not taking the lady from the *Macho Bandido* to the hospital."

The group reflected.

"You think the lady might have been saved?" Bad George asked.

Beth had overheard Billy Boy talking to Hairy Harry in her diner, saying that he thought "she'd looked dead enough for burial."

"Humph."

"Humph what?" Beth asked.

Grijpstra thought that there didn't have to be action. Not on this side, he thought. Smoking the war pipe and humphing along might just do it.

"Do what?" Lorraine asked.

"Activate Shaman *Otium Cum Dignitate.*"

"Out of office with honor," former exchange-student-in-Viareggio-Italy Lorraine translated.

"They're more dangerous that way," Grijpstra said. "You know how it goes. Doesn't he have a pretty name? So we're all agreed now?"

"Yes," Beth said.

Why Beth was boss was explained differently by different parties later. Bad George and Flash Farnsworth attributed Beth's power to her great weight. Ishmael mentioned Beth's spirit: Beth had inspired him to start the collection of What, to help cleanse *his* spirit after his release from Eastern Maine Mental. Beth was in charge of laundry at Maine Mental at the time. As she wore a white coat, some inmates thought Beth was with the psychiatric department. Beth, after hearing Ishmael out, had pronounced him normal.

"Can you imagine that?" Ishmael asked. "Me? Normal, to fly free? I tell you that was helpful."

Aki said Beth was lovable, and Lorraine said Beth was decent. Grijpstra said Beth was great. De Gier revealed a New Guinea dream he'd had during earlier training, after participating in Papuan rites. "Earth," the dream voice said, "will be saved by Big Woman."

"That's it?" Flash asked, checking the tribe's faces.

That was it.

Chapter 24

Grijpstra and de Gier watched the sea from the pagoda's porch while discussing treasure.

"Correct me if I am wrong," de Gier said, "but salt melts in water, cocaine is a more profitable product than marijuana, and Hairy Harry already has a cash-flow problem." He spread his arms. "Where does it all go? How can we put it to use?"

"First explain the salt bags," Grijpstra said.

De Gier had figured the salt out while puffing on the Algonquin war pipe. Flash had mentioned salt bags being dropped by an airplane off Rogue Island. Rogue Island was the island on Jeremy Island's far side. De Gier had seen a plane flying near Rogue Island and had noticed the sheriff's patrol boat in the area, but never at the same time as the plane. After the plane flew off, the patrol boat would arrive some six hours later. Evidently, *Kathy Three* witnessed the plane dropping bags, got wise to their procedure, got sunk for her troubles.

"The bags sank too," Grijpstra said.

De Gier's lecture continued. What happens if a bag filled with salt drops into the sea? That bag sinks. What happens once the salt melts? That bag pops up, provided contents are lighter than water. Cocaine, packed in airtight cans, is much lighter than water. If the weight of salt per bag and the speed of such weight dissolving into the ocean are given—and they are, de Gier assured the nonmathematical Grijpstra—the time that the bags, without salt, but still loaded with cocaine in airtight cans, require to surface can be figured out. Being around at that time ensures master smuggler Hairy Harry of being able to fish up the valuable cargo without being seen with the cargo-dropping plane.

"It always gets worse," Grijpstra said. "You start with a small thing, like allowing your pals to grow a little pot . . . and before you know it, you're into the big figures."

"How true," de Gier said. "Next you're destroying other people's property. Next you're destroying other people. Next you've destroyed yourself—the old Mafia merry-go-round."

"Better row me across to the diner," Grijpstra said.

"To make things enter a final stage?"

"All I ever make," Grijpstra said, "is phone calls. Maybe you know what comes next?"

"You don't want to know," de Gier said.

"Some bullshit again?" Grijpstra asked. "Some Papuan

nonsense like what you reported on while you were out in New Guinea? The tribe gathers its strong spirits together and gets them to point a bone at some subject that endangers the tribe's social health, and no matter where the subject may be, once said strong spirits are done with sitting around their campfire while chanting a ditty . . ."

"Yep," de Gier said.

Grijpstra never believed that Nellie and Katrien—please, *Nellie* and *Katrien*—humming over a leftover lamb's bone, "pointing the bone," with the commissaris leading the chant—What the hell did he chant? The Dutch national anthem?—had anything to do with subsequent mishaps that happened to kill off some parties.

Mishaps happen on the coast of Maine, especially in the Twilight Zone. Fishermen sail into the fog and stay there. Divers step into waterholes, lose their sense of direction, swim down instead of up. Hikers get eaten by blackflies in the woods. Boats burn. Seaplanes flip over. Hunters shoot each other.

Hairy Harry was shot because of Ishmael's bear mask. The foreseeable, hermit Jeremy used to say, usually doesn't occur but the unpredictable invariably happens. Aki had given the mask to Little Max. Little Max clowned around in the diner, caught the sheriff's attention, sold the mask to Hairy Harry for ten big ones. Hairy Harry and Billy Boy had a thousand-dollar bet (wagers held by Bildah Farnsworth) on who would shoot Mr. Bear. The sheriff, off duty, in his private speedboat, and Billy Boy, on duty, using the Sheriff's Office patrol boat, unbeknownst to each other, happened to choose Jeremy Island as common ground the same Sunday morning. Hairy Harry, wearing the mask and some expensive female bear scent that he had sent away for, showed his head above a rock to fool Mr. Bear and fooled Billy Boy instead. A .308 bullet, fired from Billy Boy's scoped deer rifle, pierced the mask, then messed about in the head behind it.

Billy Boy, after checking out his kill, panicked. He died later that day, pushing the patrol boat's twin engines as he raced her home to Jameson Harbor. State police officers, alerted by Billy Boy's garbled radio call that mentioned a hunting accident with one man down, waited in vain on the Jameson town dock for the sheriff's patrol to return. While Mr. Bear humped the sheriff's body, Billy Boy's boat struck rocks.

When the patrol boat didn't show, the state police chartered Big Max's lobster boat. State police detectives working with Coast Guard experts, reconstructing the accident, eventually came up with an acceptable explanation: Freak winds—Maine's infamous "cat's paws" that suddenly reach down, create havoc, and are gone again—must have shifted channel markers. The patrol boat, driven by Billy Boy, upset by accidentally shooting the sheriff, hit a shoal. The boat's hull flew over the shoal but the twin Johnson outboards were held back by solid rock. The boat could only tip over backward, had no choice but to crush her driver's body.

Grijpstra and de Gier, after one last lobster dinner, said goodbye to their fellow Algonquins and drove the Ford product to Boston's Logan Airport. Nellie met the plane in Amsterdam.

"Rinus is moving in with us, Nellie, to help with the agency. Isn't that nice?"

"Isn't it," Nellie said.

De Gier stayed in Nellie's house at Straight Tree Canal, using the gable house's loft, which he furnished with an old bath tub on a platform, a Navy hammock, and a large Oriental carpet that he found at the flea market and that Grijpstra helped him clean. Tabriz moved up with his former companion, mostly because the Grijpstra household was joined by an overactive minimongrel, soon to be named Deneuve, who followed Grijpstra home one night and declared eternal love to Nellie.

De Gier, well above all this in his loft, liked to sit in his tub and practice jazz trumpet to amuse Tabriz. Instead of reading French literature, he now borrowed South American books from the university library, which he found fascinating as, again refusing to own a dictionary, he had to guess what the Spanish or Portuguese words meant. Nellie hardly saw her unwelcome tenant as de Gier, using professional skills, managed to avoid her awesome presence. He rigged up a kitchenette, and started off each day with a ceremonial meal, enjoyed while sitting down on the carpet or, weather permitting, squatting on his small balcony in the shadow of Nellie's rooftop stone angel, bravely and forever blowing the trumpet of eternal blessings. He had his other meals out, mostly in the Chinese restaurants of Amsterdam's inner city. Massive weeds, grown from seedlings found in city alleys and on speedway shoulders, tended carefully, grew from large pots in the loft and on the balcony, where they attracted songbirds.

Chapter 25

"When we pointed the bone," Katrien had asked the commissaris the evening before Grijpstra and de Gier returned, "the party the bone points at was supposed to die?"

"I'm afraid that's correct, Katrien."

"We weren't playing?"

"No, Katrien."

"The party the bone points at dies straightaway?"

"Soon," the commissaris said.

"You really believe that?"

"Katrien," the commissaris said. "Of course I really believe that. Pointing the bone, if done properly, according to rules that de Gier left with me, is terminal magic. And we did it right. All conditions were met. We were serious. You and Nellie, in spite of what you two pretend to be sometimes, are evolved and powerful spirits. You assisted me voluntarily. The tribe requested our help and empowered our action by appropriate ritual. Of course Hairy Harry and Billy Boy terminated their temporal projections."

"How, Jan?"

"Quickly," the commissaris said.

"You sure?"

"That's what I asked for when I pointed the bone."

Katrien was knitting. The needles ticked peacefully. Sparrows chirped in the garden. An ice cream truck played its chimes in the Queen's Boulevard at the other side of the house.

"Why do you think I sent de Gier to New Guinea?" the commissaris asked.

Katrien put her knitting down. "You're arrogant, Jan. De Gier wanted to live with warriors, Papuans engaged in tribal warfare. He talked about it for years. Palm trees and jungle glades and naked women and tom-toms and halluci-nogenic plants . . ."

"I nurtured de Gier's desire on my own behalf," the commissaris said. "I couldn't go myself. I am getting too feeble."

"So de Gier is your extension?"

The commissaris sat quietly.

"I asked you a question. You're being rude."

"No," the commissaris said. "I'm too old to be rude. I want to tell you this, Katrien. I've often wondered whether there was anything we could do to make things happen a little bit better, and how far we should go once we learned how to use real power. For mutual benefit, of course."

"As defined by who?"

The commissaris sat straight in his chair, hands on his knees, eyes wide open.

"Jan?"

"Yes, Katrien."

Katrien was knitting again. Her voice was casual. "Tell me, where did Grijpstra and de Gier get all that money?"

"I think they found it, Katrien."

"Where?"

"I could tell you," the commissaris said.

"Tell me."

"I don't think it would be a good idea if you told Nellie."

"I thought Nellie was advanced and all that."

"Grijpstra should tell her himself," the commissaris said.

"I won't tell Nellie. Now tell me, Jan."

The commissaris told Katrien that he was reasonably sure the money had been found in an antique townhouse, in Amsterdam's Blood Alley, in the inner city, a little over two years ago. Grijpstra and Sergeant de Gier, who had investigated a bar in Blood Alley at that time, announced their resignation a few days later.

"An investigation to do with a body?" Katrien asked.

With a missing body, a Japanese tourist, who later turned up safe and sound. The found Japanese missing person liked to drink in a Blood Alley bar.

"You followed up?"

The commissaris shrugged. Of course he followed up. Didn't he just love mysteries? His very own trusted assistants, suddenly resigning, citing that as he, the commissaris, was about to be pensioned off, they couldn't stay on. "A likely story, Katrien."

"I thought it was touching, Jan."

"Grijpstra retiring on his savings? A couple of hundreds? And de Gier on his inheritance from his mother? A couple of thousands? Next thing Grijpstra is remodeling Nellie's house and de Gier is off to New Guinea."

"I remember," Katrien said. "You were running about in your father's broad-brimmed felt hat and Uncle Piet's little round glasses and that oversize overcoat you found in the garbage and you smelled of jenever when you came home late." Katrien sniffed. "Retired, ha! *Otium cum dignitate* indeed." She found her smile again. "So what happened in Blood Alley that made millionaires out of our musketeers?"

Information is found in bars. The commissaris told her that while illegally investigating his former associates' sudden wealth, he had visited the bar in Blood Alley, assuming the persona of a retired city clerk, a drinking man, sitting quietly at the counter, hearing the alley's seasoned drinkers discussing a house further along the alley, about to be impounded for nonpayment of taxes, where three middle-aged black males used to live, citizens of Suriname, a former Dutch colony on the South American East Coast. The three men drove Maseratis that were traded for new Maseratis as soon as ashtrays filled up or tape decks malfunctioned. A

Maserati is a very expensive Italian brand of sports car. Those citizens of the republic of Suriname, a very poor country, just loved driving their ever-new Maseratis.

"Subjects left their station, Jan?"

Nobody had answered the door of the Blood Alley house. The telephone had been disconnected. The cars, abandoned and vandalized, were still in the alley. Grijpstra and de Gier had had the vehicles towed to Headquarters. A search turned up unpaid traffic tickets. The Maseratis were auctioned off by the city.

"The owners didn't show?"

No. The commissaris, at that time, recalled a narcotics case that mentioned the Maserati owners as suspects.

"Suspected of what, Jan?"

Of importing frozen fruit juice that wasn't. The product hidden in the fruit juice cans was cocaine. Strangely enough, the alleged smugglers were heroin users. Suspects had been brought in on charges a few times but released for lack of police cells, a common Amsterdam problem, but they were still being harassed by detectives, asked to visit Headquarters to answer questions, waylaid in the street, telephoned at odd times.

"Aha," Katrien said.

"You see possibilities?" the commissaris asked.

"Panic?" Katrien asked. "The addicted Suriname suspects, driven crazy by being constantly under surveillance, ran home? Leaving their treasure?"

The commissaris confirmed that addicts often react

erratically because of the narcotics side effect, paranoia. Having come that far, the commissaris had asked a former Murder Brigade assistant, Sergeant-Detective Simon Cardozo, to check with Suriname, where the Dutch Ministry of Justice pays off informers. There was a rumor in Suriname's capital that the three suspects were arrested by the military police on their return to Paramaribo. The rumor said that the military police, who handled the "frozen fruit juice" flow from Suriname to Amsterdam, wanted their share of the profits. The three suspects hadn't brought any money with them. They were tortured inefficiently and died before they could tell the MPs where the Amsterdam treasure, the proceeds of sales of narcotics, was hidden.

"Ach," Katrien said. "And Grijpstra and de Gier found the lost millions? Hidden in that Blood Alley house? Oh dear."

The commissaris said fortunes in cash left by drug dealers had been found by his department before and had been turned over to the administration.

"Aha," Katrien said. "Yes, I remember. You thought the money either disappeared outright or got squandered somehow."

The commissaris sighed as he held her hand. The old couple thought about the declining police reputation, unreported serious crimes, killer psychopaths released for bureaucratic reasons, unemployed youth gangs robbing the weak and elderly. Katrien was shaking her head. "So Grijpstra and de Gier just kept the cash? And you approve?"

"Not really, dear."

"You'll make them hand in the treasure somehow? But they're spending the money, Jan. There won't be much left."

The commissaris shook his head. "The treasure has been growing, dear."

"So it's you again," Katrien said. "How come you're always behind every mystery I run into? So that's what you've been advising Grijpstra about. All that talk about investments. I couldn't figure it out, why you were discussing shares and foreign exchange and interest and whatnot with Grijpstra of all people. Oh dear, oh dear."

"I was always good with numbers," the commissaris said. "I almost doubled the original value of Grijpstra's haul."

Katrien gaped.

The commissaris smiled proudly. "That's after what they were both spending is deducted, of course. We did well with the dollar's fluctuation. I bought and sold Deutsche Marks then, and buying Philips at nineteen and selling at over thirty helped too, of course. Then there was Gillette. We went short on gold for a bit. We also bet that the British Labor Party would lose, so that the British Stock Index would go up, and, Katrien, didn't it ever?" He shook his head. "It's all in bonds now. I'm out of inspiration, but there's twice as much as there was."

"What if those two start spending again?" Katrien asked. "Nellie says de Gier is buying a car."

The commissaris shrugged. "An old Citroën Deux

Chevaux. Something he can leave in the street without its getting stolen. The agency makes good money, I hear. By now they're eager to get rid of their burden."

"You have something in mind?"

"Don't know yet, dear. Support the buccaneers who shoot up whalers? Give away anticonception devices in starving nations? Advertise euthanasia and sterilization? Help NASA to transport Homo sapiens to faraway places, one way? You know of something better?"

"Hospitals for crippled kids," Katrien said. "I'll do some research, find us an organization where the staff isn't off on donation-supported cruises."

"Katrien?" the commissaris asked later that day. "I have this leaflet here, about this cruise. It's a small vessel belonging to some biological society, quite luxurious, with staterooms, leaving next month. Bird watching. On the coast of Maine. And as I've been feeling much better lately . . . all we have to do is catch a Concorde."

Chapter 26

           Some weeks later a rubber boat was lowered down the side of the biological cruise ship *Lazy Loon,* out of New York, now anchored in Jameson Bay, Maine. Autumn was almost over, and the boat's passenger wore a sheepskin coat. He wasn't Katrien's favorite person that day but she could still stand at the *Lazy Loon*'s railing and wave down at him.

    The rubber boat's operator, a marine biology student, insisted on showing his passenger harbor seals, a gray seal, the dorsal fins of dolphins, an immature bald eagle, a jellyfish, and two loons, before dropping him off at Beth's Diner.

    "Akiapola'au?" the commissaris asked as she brought him a menu. He mentioned his last name.

    "That's Algonquin?" Aki asked. "But you have a Dutch accent. You must be the chief from Amsterdam. How are Rinus and Krip? Beth! Look who we have here."

Beth brought blueberry muffins on the house.

Aki and Beth sat at his table. "We are going to Hawaii soon."

"For good?" the commissaris asked.

"Just to winter a while," Aki said. "We can afford to now. Are you going to see what Ishmael has done with his canning factory? All those colors and corridors and depth and 'perspectives.' Something about emptiness and space. If you get it, will you tell us?"

"Bad George?" the commissaris asked. "Flash Farnsworth?"

Beth brought more muffins and filtered Kona coffee. "The *Kathy Four* is sailing down Eggemoggin Reach just now, Flash radioed in. They're going mackerel fishing. Ishmael flew down yesterday. His new Cessna has sea floats. There'll be the three of them there, sharing good times."

"The four of them," the commissaris said.

The women laughed. "You've been told about Kathy Two?"

Kathy Two was doing just fine.

"Lorraine?" the commissaris asked.

Lorraine was back in New York, lecturing on her loon research. She was seeing her former husband, who was telling her about his wife. She was seeing his wife too.

"Bildah Farnsworth?"

Beth drove the commissaris to Bildah Farnsworth's hilltop residence, formerly the property of Hairy Harry.

Bildah was home. Beth introduced the commissaris. "You two should talk," Beth said. She drove off.

Bildah, a small-sized older man with neat sharp features, faded blue eyes behind rimless glasses, bald under his felt hat, and wearing a sheepskin jacket ("You know, we look alike?"), took the commissaris for a walk.

"You know," Bildah said, "when someone is indicted here, he always says, 'I didn't do anything wrong.' "

"I'm not indicting you," the commissaris said.

Bildah looked glum. "You might still be my conscience."

The commissaris explained his theory about conscience, that it was a fickle thing, tied loosely together by the strings of habit and memory, inflicted by impressions received early on in life, far too relative to be trusted.

"You're retired, I hear," Bildah said. "I had you checked out somewhat. You knew our previous sheriff, Jim. Jim spoke highly of you. He became a game warden, you know, in the Florida Keys. Trying to protect some small type of deer that gets hit by traffic."

"Good," the commissaris said, "and I'm glad you think you did nothing wrong."

They walked slowly, to keep time with the commissaris's limp, under maples in autumn colors along a picket fence overgrown with scarlet vines. Jameson Bay was below. "A beautiful place," the commissaris said.

Bildah nodded. "We are lucky." He touched the commissaris's sleeve. "Technically I did nothing wrong either."

"The lady was dead when she was found in the *Macho Bandido*'s cabin?" the commissaris asked.

"Hairy Harry said so." Bildah looked out over the bay where the yacht was tied up to a mooring. "I didn't want the *Bandido* then so he registered the boat in his own name. I never saw the lady."

"The boat is in your name now?"

It was. Bildah explained that Hairy Harry had been married and was childless. His widow had wanted to cut her ties and go. She sold the house to Bildah.

"For what Hairy Harry paid you? Half its value?"

It was more than what the sheriff's widow had expected. Bildah didn't pay much for the *Macho Bandido* either. All the widow wanted was out. Things always came to Bildah that way—investments, property, deals. "I don't even have to put out my hand," said Bildah.

"You accept all bounty?" the commissaris asked pleasantly.

"You bet." Bildah smiled. "As they say—living well is the best revenge. You're rich yourself?"

The commissaris excused his own luck. "Rich wife, good wages, a pension, lucky with numbers."

They looked at hills on the horizon.

"I don't believe in guilt," Bildah said. "I believe in philosophical curiosity, and in putting things together so as to enjoy some simple comforts, in continuity, for the duration, so to speak."

The commissaris looked down at Jameson Bay, the

islands, the foliage in color, the endless ocean, the yacht ready to sail.

"You picked a good spot."

"I should be sailing now," Bildah said, "I wanted to take a look at your cruise ship today but Little Max had to go to the dentist and I have trouble handling *Macho Bandido* alone."

They walked on. "Your men did a good job here," Bildah said. "Hairy Harry and Billy Boy were hiding a lot of cash. Your men must have told Ishmael and friends where they should look. The dead men's treasure made up for all pain and losses."

"The tunnel on Jeremy Island, guarded by the corpse and Mr. Bear?" the commissaris asked.

Bildah thought that was the location.

"A lot of money?"

Quite a fortune, Bildah thought. Sudden wealth can be destructive but Ishmael could probably handle sudden wealth. Ishmael was quite special; it seemed he shared the loot to everybody's satisfaction. Ishmael himself only wanted to replace his airplane.

"You're not sorry the treasure didn't end up with you?"

Bildah smiled, said he had enough to carry on with, thank you, and wasn't it nice to have rich neighbors? Flash had bought him a lobster dinner last time they met.

"What about the salt bags concealing cocaine and the marijuana shipments?"

"Big Max is arranging to take over," Bildah said. "The new sheriff may put a stop to that."

"Take it over himself?"

Bildah didn't think so. The new sheriff came from law enforcement in a Boston ghetto, he didn't care for drugs. If he stayed honest, the business would have to move up north.

"A question," the commissaris said. "Why didn't you back up Hairy Harry? You were here and I was a long way out. You could have protected him and Billy Boy, yes?"

Bildah was quiet.

"You must have felt something was up." The commissaris took time to divulge recent doings: the ritual with Nellie and Katrien.

"A lamb's bone," Bildah said. "So that works, does it? I always thought that sort of thing would. I've read about pointing the bone. Australian aborigines do it. I didn't know the custom had also spread to New Guinea. It's dangerous, right?"

"Never fails." The commissaris nodded. "Kills your victim."

Bildah nodded too. "Yes, sure, but what I read is that the force evoked and released, the power, the devil if you will, may turn halfway and kill the pointer."

"If the gods don't agree?" The commissaris shrugged. "The gods must be environmentalists these days."

"Challenge the subconscious?" Bildah was impressed.

"What's to lose?" the commissaris asked. "Don't mind dying myself." He stopped and faced his host. "Now, tell me, were you aware that your men were in danger?"

Bildah was.

"So why didn't you protect Hairy Harry?" the commissaris asked again.

"I didn't want to," Bildah said.

The two old men sat on rocks, quietly taking in the view.

"Hairy Harry who, by the way, never was *my man,* as you put it," Bildah said, "was clever in some little ways, a minor god in a minor universe, but abysmal ignorance made him shoot Croakie."

Croakie, Bildah said, had been a good raven. Bildah had raised Croakie from the time he was a chick who had either fallen or been pushed from his nest. Croakie was blind in one eye and lame in one leg and would sit on Bildah's shoulder. "I have no family," Bildah said. "Man is designed to be gregarious, to interact with fellow beings. So I sometimes feel lonely." He turned to the commissaris. "You have company yourself?"

The commissaris mentioned Katrien and Turtle.

Bildah didn't know about wives or reptiles but he and Croakie had been close. Croakie would fly upside down to make Bildah laugh. Croakie could pronounce four-letter words thoughtfully. "Croakie was free, of course. He had his own window that he knew how to open so that he could sleep in my room."

Bildah said that the sheriff and his deputy's frequent beer-drinking parties sometimes gave way to killing sprees. The two would fire at sparrows, sea gulls, Croakie.

"You don't hunt yourself?" the commissaris asked.

"Not since Korea." Bildah was in the war there. He had been a medic.

"You don't mind drugs?"

"Don't care for them myself," Bildah said. "But we should make them legal, don't you think?"

The commissaris thought that might happen at some date in the future, if there still was one.

Bildah drove the commissaris back to the harbor.

"Did Akiapola'au look as billed?" Katrien asked, helping him up the cruise vessel's steep gangway. "Are we going to Hawaii now?"

That evening in their stateroom, while the *Lazy Loon* moved in a leisurely fashion on Jameson Bay's slow swell, under a full and quiet moon, listening to loons chuckling near Squid island, the commissaris said that he would never understand it.

"Understand what, Jan?"

The commissaris said that he would never understand the beauty.

"Of this?"

"Of it all."

About the Author

Janwillem van de Wetering was born in Rotterdam in 1931, studied Zen in Daitoku-ji Monastery, Kyoto and philosophy in London, and has lived as well in Amsterdam, Cornwall, Capetown, Bogota, Lima, and Brisbane. In 1975 he settled in a small town on the coast of Maine where he still lives.

The Amsterdam Cops series that features Adjutant Grijpstra and Sergeant de Gier working as extensions of the commissaris, a wily and philosophical Amsterdam Chief of Detectives, was conceived when the author served with the Amsterdam Reserve Constabulary. To date over two million copies of his works are in print in fourteen languages.

His joys are an ongoing study of nihilism, keeping a wooden lobster boat afloat and getting older. His pain is an inability to play the jazz trumpet.

He has been married for a long time, no longer smokes or drinks, is kept by a superior dog (like the one in this story), and has become allergic to the guru syndrome.